Ready to Run

NOT BESTSELLING AUTHORS

JENNIFER REBECCA
ALYSSA KALE

Ready to Run

Copyright © 2021 Jennifer Rebecca & Alyssa Kale

Cover and Formatting: Alyssa Garcia
Editor: Kayla Robichaux
Proofreader: Karin Enders

Ready to Run

READY TO RUN

Bayleigh Hart

RELATIONSHIP STATUS: *Runaway Bride*

I didn't mean to. It just happened. I swear it. One minute, I was walking down the aisle, and the next, I was in Bora Bora with my bestie, Archer Scott. But this honeymoon isn't in Vegas, and the feelings and naked parts we discovered aren't going to stay there.

Archer Scott

RELATIONSHIP STATUS: *In love with my best friend.*

I always thought I would have time to get closer to Bayleigh. That was until I was checking the Yes box on the RSVP for her wedding. One minute, she's about to begin her life with Mr. Not Me, and the next, I'm dancing on a bar in a grass skirt. Fortunately, I'm a "grab the bull by the horns" kind of guy, so I go with it.

It's like they always say—Shh… it happens!

PROLOGUE

OH CRAP

Bayleigh

There's a conga drum beat in my head, and it feels like the time I forgot a Tupperware of noodles on the floorboard of my car and it became penicillin and then crawled up and died on my tongue. I swallow back the acid that's crawling up my throat, and I grit my teeth against the wave of nausea that hits me like a ton of bricks.

Apparently, the Mai Tais were really flowing last night.

I vaguely remember Archer wearing a grass skirt and dancing on a bar top… and then dancing with me? The memories flit through my mind of me in his arms and his hips pressed to mine, the feel of his hard length against my belly. But that can't be right, *right?*

I should definitely avoid the worm in the bottom of the tequila bottles, because holy hallucinogenic dreams, Batman!

But then a strong arm snakes under the sheet and around my belly—*my naked belly*—and a heavy hand falls to my bare breast. Holy shit! I'm naked! And there's a man in my bed.

I don't remember going home with anyone last night, but arguably, I drank too much. As it was our last night in Bora Bora, Archer and I decided to live it up before we took our happy asses back to East Texas to get on with my life post-breakup.

He was supposed to be my wingman on this trip, and somehow he let down his guard. My bestie let a fox in the hen house, and I guess now I'm going to have to woman-up and find out just who it is.

I take a deep breath, shore up my courage, and turn my head. I follow the masculine hand with neatly trimmed nails up the lean forearm that's dusted with a light sprinkling of dark hair. A few veins follow the path of the muscles and tendons as they tell their story up to biceps cut with thick muscles. Broad shoulders go on to a corded neck and chiseled jawline with a dark shadow….

Wait… a familiar jawline.

I look down at what's underneath the sheets. *That's*

some fox in the hen house.
Oh crap. What did I do?

ONE

MAN OF HONOR

Archer

Ten Days Earlier

"**A**re you ready?" I ask Bayleigh when I step into the bridal room after she's finished putting on the most beautiful dress I've ever seen—fitted but flowy and hugs her body in the perfect spots, without it being overly sexy.

And of course it's white. There is no other color for this day for Bay. She looks like a bride. *Probably because she is a bride.* That's like a fist to my gut. I never thought we'd be here like this. I thought we had more time. I thought *I* had more time.

She half smiles and nods. "Yeah, I think so."

There is a twinge of uncertainty in her voice, and I'm not sure why. She has planned for this day since we were little kids. A small hometown wedding with just her family and her closest friends. She always wanted to wear her mom's veil and carry her grandfather's hankie. Every detail, she had planned like I guess all little girls do when they daydream.

Her dad will be in here any minute. He's making sure his mom gets to her seat before the ceremony starts.

"The wedding planner said you could have one shot of vodka or tequila before the ceremony starts," I say, holding both travel bottles up in a "this one" or "that one" way.

"Oh, yes please," she breathes out. "I'll take the vodka. Tequila makes me sick after that one night in college." Her face pulls into a ridiculous grimace that makes me laugh.

I don't know what she's talking about, since she left for the coast while I was still in my undergrad years, and that's one story she's never told me. I make a mental note to ask her about it later. I laugh with her, open the vodka bottle, and hand it to her. She puts it to her lips and tilts her head back, taking it down like it's water. Without a chaser. Well, okay then. Bayleigh always was a wild one.

"You really are beautiful, Bay," I tell her with a smile on my face. Even if it's not genuine, the sentiment is. She's the most beautiful woman I've ever laid eyes on.

She comes in for a hug. "Thank you so much for being here and for being my man of honor."

"I wouldn't miss this day for the world." I wish things were different, but it's not a lie. I wish it were me waiting for her outside, but instead, she's about to marry the biggest douche of them all.

Well, he's a douche to me. Her fiancé, Dr. Paul Jacobs, keeps calling me Archie, 'cause he knows it pisses me off. What kind of name is Paul Jacobs? One that belongs to the douchey plastic surgeon to the stars. I mentally roll my eyes. When I met him, he told me that he was known for his nose and ass work. Like, what the fuck was that about? I told him I was known for my ass work too, seeing as I had just delivered a breech donkey, but apparently, I was the only one who thought that was funny.

Don't ruin this day for Bayleigh. Don't ruin this day for Bayleigh. I run the words over and over in my head and pray like fuck that they stick.

Paul is a plastic surgeon to the stars and hired Bayleigh when she was a struggling actress trying to make it in the world of Hollywood. He ended up hooking her up with one of his clients who is an agent, and lately, her career seems to be taking off. She just finished filming a major book adaptation that already has a huge following, and people are stalking her social media accounts, even though it hasn't been released yet.

The other day, she was on the cover of a grocery store tabloid getting a burrito at Chipotle. I couldn't believe it. I had to call her right away and tell her to get her skinny ass back to Texas if she thought Chipotle makes a decent burrito. But I digress.

She lets go of me when her mom, Alivia Hart, walks through the door. She swipes at the bottom of her eye, almost like she was crying a little. Her mom loves Paul. I have no idea why.

"Your dad will be here in just a few minutes, baby. Are you ready?"

"I am. Do you think he'll like it, Mom?" she asks nervously as she twirls around so her mom can see her full wedding look.

"I have no doubt, honey." Liv has tears running down her cheeks that she begins to pat with a tissue. "You're so beautiful."

They had their moment earlier when she helped Bayleigh put the dress on, but Mrs. Hart is still super emotional, and she has every right to be; her baby girl is getting married.

Before any more words can be exchanged, there's a knock at the door.

"Everyone decent?" her dad asks when he cracks it open slightly.

"Yeah, Dad, come in," Bayleigh says, more chipper than just a few minutes ago.

The photographer in the room begins snapping the

shutter on the camera, capturing the moment her dad sees her in her dress for the first time. Apparently, she's been in here for a while and probably got some images of our moment too, but I was too wrapped up in Bayleigh to notice.

"Oh, Bayleigh." He takes a deep breath to keep the emotion from bubbling up. "You look so beautiful."

"You think so, Dad?" She smiles.

"I know so, darlin'." He places his hand on his heart while she turns, showing him the dress. It has pieces of her mom's dress. Someone had spilled red wine down the front of it on their wedding day, so it couldn't be worn, but being sentimental, Alivia saved it anyway, and I know Bayleigh loves having pieces of it with her today. "You look just like your mom."

"Love you, Daddy."

He's speechless now, and it really is a beautiful moment. It's the moment a father realizes his little girl is grown up and he now has to share her with another man. I can see the emotion going through his eyes. He's so proud of her but doesn't want to take the next step just yet.

He'll be giving her away in less than thirty minutes, but what no one else knows is he's not the only one giving her away. I am too. After today, Bayleigh will have another man in her life—for the rest of her life. One who takes much more priority over me. She's going to be Paul's, and the thought sours my stomach like homemade hooch.

Unable to take anymore, I clear my throat, and when she looks at me, I walk to her. "I'm going to head out there. I'll see you in a few."

"Thank you for being here, Ace."

She grabs my hand and pulls me into one last hug. As much as I want to tell her not to do this, tell her that the man she's about to marry is a jackass, I don't. She's smiling and happy now, and I'm not going to be the one to take that away from her.

"I wouldn't do this for anyone else; don't forget that." I point at her, making light of the heavy emotions in the room.

"Trust me, you'll never let me forget." She laughs. "At least you're not in a lavender dress."

"Hell no, I won't let you forget my awesomeness in this moment." I smirk. "See you out there."

"I'll be the one in white." She winks.

Oh, don't I know it. My heart twists and turns painfully in my chest.

A few minutes later, I'm making my way toward the spot I was told to wait for the ceremony to start. Paul, his best man, and his groomsmen are standing and joking around. They don't see me until I'm about six feet from them.

"Oh look, it's Archie the 'doctor,'" Paul sneers, putting the last word in air quotes and saying it like it's an insult. Apparently, being a doctor for animals is a joke to them. Personally, I like my animals more. They're usually more well-mannered than these assholes.

I roll my eyes; it's not worth trying to fight these guys. I went to one of the best veterinary schools in the country before coming home to take over my dad's practice so he could retire when he was ready. Just because I don't spend my day telling women they aren't perfect to sell them plastic upgrades doesn't make me less-than. If anything, I'm more of a man, because I know what to do with a real woman, curves and all. I bet these dickheads always finish first. The thought brings a smirk to my mouth.

"Cat got your tongue, buddy?" His best man asks as they all snicker.

"Stop it, boys," an older lady comes up and reprimands them. "This is your wedding, Paul, and this is your bride's best friend. Be nice."

"Yes, Mother," Paul says, embarrassed because he just got reamed by Mommy.

I bite my tongue to hold back my laugh and shift over to my spot and wait for the music to start the walk to the altar.

Before long, the rest of the guests take their seats at the instruction of the wedding planner. She takes a moment to remind everyone that this is a technology-free ceremony and no phones will be allowed out, to just enjoy watching. The photographers will capture the best moments.

The music starts, and we make our way to our places, following the mothers and grandmothers as they are escorted in.

Eventually, the lone bridesmaid, my sister, Evan, makes her way down the aisle before the super-cute ringbearer and flower girl make their dissent. I'm so distracted by the kids' cuteness that I don't see everyone stand up for the bride, but when the song switches from *Canon in D* to the traditional wedding march, I look up and see the doors open.

When Bayleigh comes into view, I feel my heart begin to break into a million pieces. I'm not sure why I suddenly feel like this. Maybe it's just the significance of the day. Or maybe it's because there actually is something more between us and I'm just now noticing it.

I'm not even sorry there aren't hot bridesmaids here, because after today, I'm not going to want to get my dick wet. I'm going to need a bottle of tequila.

Bayleigh finally looks up, and instead of staring straight at her groom… she looks at me. She looks at me in a way that sinks directly into my soul. She's the most beautiful bride I've ever seen.

I smile at her when I catch her eyes, and she smiles back. It's like no one else in the room exists. It's just Bayleigh and me. The way it's supposed to be. The way it always should've been. It's like all the pieces have finally clicked into place.

But it was never meant to be.

What are you doing, Bayleigh? Don't do this. I will her to hear my thoughts, my pleas. I need her to hear the words we've never spoken.

She continues to walk, and I lose every ounce of hope I have that fate is going to deliver me a sign. I can't change things now. I'm not that guy.

She's going to marry Paul, and there is nothing I can do about it. It's too late. I've lost her.

I have to remember she's not here for me.

TWO

Bayleigh

I'm fine. This is fine. *Everything is fine*. There is no need to panic. I feel like that's akin to calling the Titanic just a little bit of rocky sailing.

Spoiler alert: Everything is not fine. Nope. Not even a little bit. This ship is sinking fast, and I need to find my lifejacket and a lifeboat with room for one. Definitely one.

Why is that? Why do we women always say that everything is fine when it absolutely is *not* fine? I will never know. What I really need is to stop doing that to myself. I need to just accept things are not okay and move on instead of planning and following through with a very expensive wedding to the absolute wrong man. Maybe in my next life, I'll be more like Evan, Archer's sister. She says exactly what she's thinking, usually to the point that she shouldn't have said anything at all, but hey, at least everyone knows how she feels. There's no stewed-on and bottled-up feelings there.

And how do I feel?

I feel like I've fallen overboard in the middle of the ocean and don't know who I am or where I belong. It's kind of like that Goldie Hawn movie, *Overboard*. I love that freaking movie. And man, can I relate right now. Am I Bayleigh Hart of Sunnyville, Texas, a small-town girl who once set off a buck bomb in my boyfriend's car because I caught him making out with MaryAnne Watkins behind the football field? Or am I Bayleigh Hart of Hollywood, sometimes actress, mostly a receptionist with one big movie under my belt that has yet to be released?

"You ready?" my dad asks me when the music changes, and I barely resist the urge to ask him if he knows, because I sure as shit do not. I love that phrase—sure as shit. It's just one of the things Paul doesn't like about me. He wants me to be less Texas and more SoCal. Like it's a choice or something. I hate that he cringes when I say things like buggy instead of shopping cart or Coke instead of soda. And the way he rolls his eyes if I drop a "y'all" or a "fixin' to" is downright rude. I mean, does he even like me?

I smile the smile that landed me a toothpaste print ad and link my arm with Dad's, transferring my bouquet to my right hand. Fake it 'til you make it, right?

"You look just like your mom," he tells me again, and I can hear the little catch in his throat. Emotion isn't something we Harts wear well. Mom likes to say we're all emotionally stunted, and truth be told, she's probably not that far off the mark.

"Really?"

"Oh yeah, you have her smile," he says, and then I can't be totally sure because he says it so quietly, but I think he mutters, "And that same stupid look on your face when you're full of shit."

"What was that?" I ask.

"I said 'I think this is our cue,'" he lies.

Whatever. I've got this. I've totally got this. There is no need to panic. I think I said that already.

The doors open, and we step out onto the white runner that will lead me to my future. Paul loves me. He wants to marry me. He wants to be my forever.

But a little voice in the back of my mind whispers, *If he wants to be your forever, then why was his nurse texting him at your rehearsal dinner?*

We were sitting at our table at the small Mexican cantina, the multicolored glass tea light holders twinkling on the tabletops. The smell of spices from the delicious food clung invitingly to the air of the outdoor patio surrounded by trees, a stucco wall, and a gate that make you feel like you're eating with family in someone's backyard. I love that restaurant. It's my absolute favorite besides the tavern a town over.

Paul had just gotten up from the table to grab another round of the dangerous margaritas, when his phone buzzed on the metal tabletop. I picked it up without thinking. Having been his receptionist, I was used to answering his phones and email of all varieties. Honestly, having done it for so long, I'm surprised he himself can text. Almost as surprised as I was to find out his nurse was texting him pictures of her own pink kitty cat as a wedding present.

AMY: hey baby are you done with your thing?

"Your thing" meaning the rehearsal for our wedding? *Uhh… what now?*

AMY: call me when you're done. I miss you.

Maybe the office was boring without patients. Maybe there was nothing on TV. I could make up a hundred excuses, but I knew it then and I know it now—Paul is a creep, and Amy is a ho.

I had scrolled up through their conversation over the past few days that he'd been in Texas for our prenuptial festivities, and it looked like ole Amy had been chatty. And she sent pictures!

But Paul wouldn't cheat, right?

I had lain in bed with him and told him how much it hurt me when my high school sweetheart cheated on me before prom. I ended up going with Archer, who dumped his date to take me because he felt so bad. She was not excited about that. Archer was a catch back in high school. Football running back in the fall, and third baseman in the spring. He probably could have played professionally if he wanted, but his heart was in saving animals. I still don't know why he's single.

Why would Paul be texting Amy? That didn't even make any sense. We were getting married. I don't know what possessed me to do it—maybe it was a little bit of self-preservation, I don't know. I screenshot their conversation, texted the photos to my own phone, and then deleted all the screenshots and the text to me before placing the phone back where I found it on the tabletop.

Now, my dad and I take another step, and my eyes lock on Archer. Sweet, funny, hot-as-hell Archer. How I had always hoped that one day he'd just notice me. Not as his friend, but as… more.

But it was never meant to be.

How I wish it were him I was walking to and not Paul. Even if Paul probably wasn't banging his nurse, I'd still wish it was Archer. Gosh, I've loved him since I was eight years old, and he never realized it. He never saw the way I looked for him in every room, or the way my heart would break just a little every time he introduced me to yet another girl he was dating.

Besides, I love Paul.

I don't love Paul, do I?

And this might be the vodka talking, but he's really banging his nurse, isn't he?

Shit. I think he's been cheating on me. How could he do this? He knew. He knew how much I couldn't stand cheating. And he did it anyway. After everything we had together and all I shared with him, he still dipped his wick where it didn't belong.

Goddammit. I'm not okay. I can't do this.

Shit.

My eyes flash from Archer to Paul, and I stop in my tracks. My dad, not with the change in program yet, continues his forward momentum and almost knocks me over before he stops a step ahead of me and looks back, confusion written all over his face.

"Bayleigh?"

"Oh shit," Evan says. "She looks like she's ready to run."

"Bayleigh?" Paul asks.

"I think she finally figured out her fiancé is fucking whoever it is he keeps texting all the time," Evan announces, and I close my eyes tight. I can't believe even my friends noticed things with Paul weren't quite right. But why didn't they say anything? Why did they all let me believe the lies?

"What?" Paul prompts just a little too quickly. "That's not true."

But isn't it though? I let out a frustrated sigh and maybe a tiny burp. Vodka always did give me the worst indigestion.

"Bayleigh?" my mom asks. "What's going on?"

"I can't do this."

"What?" Mom gasps.

At the same time, I swear my dad mutters, "Thank fuck."

"Bayleigh? Are you fucking kidding me?" Paul bites out. "You can't possibly believe that."

"But he's a doctor," my mom wails. I like how that's the selling point she can't let go of. Eventually, when the dust clears, she'll realize that life with Paul and his infidelities would eventually break me. Better break it off now than end up in therapy later, I guess.

"He's an asshole, Liv," Dad replies. "I only wish she figured that out before it cost me twenty grand."

"This isn't about the money, Henry," Mom snaps, clearly unhappy she's losing her grip on the lifelong vision of a doctor for a son-in-law.

"It's a lot of fucking money," Dad says, and really, he's not wrong. I kind of want to throw up thinking about twenty thousand dollars down the shitter.

"Bayleigh, stop this shit right now," Paul commands.

"No." My eyes go wide, and so do everyone else's. I'm pretty sure no one—*including me*—thought I would tell Paul no. But I can't help it. Once the word is out of my mouth, I know the truth.

"You can't possibly believe her. I mean, who is she anyway?" he asks, trying to draw suspicions on one of my best friends. Evan, Asher, and I were practically raised together like a pack of feral cats. I trust Evan with my life. "She's a nobody."

"Now excuse me," Evan's mom, Mary, butts in. "I know you're upset right now, but that's no excuse for rudeness."

"Fuck this, and fuck you," Paul bites out, and I can't let him continue talking to the people I love like that. It's time to choose who I'm going to be and where I belong, and it's with these people, not Paul.

"She's one of my oldest friends," I answer. "And yeah, I do believe her."

"What?" he gripes. "There will be no going back once you make this choice."

"You don't love me, Paul, and I don't think I love you. Not like I should."

"You'll regret this," he snaps.

"Maybe," I say, shrugging my shoulders and feeling like a huge weight has been lifted off of them for the first time in a long time. "Then again, maybe not. Say hi to Amy for me."

"Bayleigh?" Archer approaches me. "Everything all right?"

"Well hey there, good buddy." I smile my I'm-so-innocent smile at him that he always knew was bullshit but went along with my schemes anyways. "Funny you should mention it. But I happen to be in need of a quick getaway."

"Well, never fear." He chuckles as he takes my hand. "I just so happen to have one."

"Dammit, Bayleigh!" Paul shouts, and my mom cries, but my dad, he just throws his head back and laughs.

And then we run back down the aisle and out of the church. What happens next, I have no fucking idea, but with my bestie by my side, I know it'll all be okay.

THREE

FAST CAR

Archer

'm holding onto Bayleigh's hand, weaving my way through the parking lot to get to my car. I brought my 1969 Mercury Comet. It's not my drive-everywhere vehicle—that's my old truck—this is for special occasions. I save her for moments that mean something, whether good or bad, and today was gearing up to be one of those days.

Being the true gentleman I am, I let go of her hand and jog quickly in front of her to make sure I open her door before she can even try. My momma didn't raise an asshole, that's for sure. Besides, I have to take care of my girl.

My girl?

I'm sure I'll process that later, but until then, I need to get her someplace safe so she can decompress and just be okay. I need her to be okay.

When we make it to the car, we hear Paul yelling from the building he just walked out of, "Bayleigh, stop being such a dumb bitch."

On instinct, I turn around to go punch the shit out of this jackass, but Bayleigh grabs my arm and shakes her head.

"Let's just get out of here, okay?" She doesn't look mad or sad but instead defeated. Like his being a jerk is her fault. It makes me wonder what the actual fuck was going on in Los Angeles all this time. I need to know what happened, but I also know now isn't the time. Now, I need to diffuse this situation so I can protect Bayleigh and get her out of here safely. I don't know this man, not really, or what he's capable of, and I shouldn't underestimate him in this volatile moment.

I nod as she slides into the passenger seat, struggling with her puffy dress. It balloons all around her, and in any other situation, I would laugh my ass off, but right now, not so much. I help her shove it in before shutting the door. I turn back around and take four long, angry strides back toward the asshole who hurt my friend and punch him in the face. I shake out my hand as blood spurts from his nose and make my way around to the driver side.

Once I'm safely in, seat belt and all, I crank the engine and rev it a few times. Douchebag Paul is almost to my vehicle and looks like he's going to move in and reach for the door handle, but with one look at the scowl on my face, he knows I mean business and backs off. He's pissed and clearly cussing, but we can't hear him over the engine.

When we've made our way away from the crowd, I pick up speed before getting to the end of the driveway, and that's when I really hit the gas and hear the tires kick up some gravel from the road. After making sure there's no traffic ahead of us, I peel out in front of her family, my family, and Paul's. It probably isn't my best moment, but who cares? I can't put the toothpaste back in the tube now.

I'm worried what Bayleigh will think. Is she mad at me for hitting that jerk? I can't believe he'd speak to her like that. Does he treat her like that all the time? There's a burning pit in my stomach. I'm not sure I want to know the answer to that, but I need to. If he ever took a hand to her, I'm going to break his fucking fingers. But when I glance over at Bay, I know I needn't have worried at all. She's wearing the most beautiful carefree smile on her face—just like when we were kids. Her blonde hair is blowing in the breeze.

"Where to now?" I ask.

She ponders for a minute, then smiles slyly. "Well, I booked and prepaid for the honeymoon. Hang on, let me see your phone. I left mine back in the bride's dressing room."

I dig into my suit pocket for my phone and hand it to her. "Here."

She unlocks it with the code I've used for years and searches for something. When she finds what she's looking for, she says, "Ah-ha!"

"What?" I ask hesitantly. If there's one thing I know for sure, it's that look on her face means nothing but trouble. And I want it—I crave it. Whatever she's selling, I'm buying, because in this moment, this very second, I would sell my soul to put that glimmer back in her eyes. I would do anything to make her happy.

"For two-hundred dollars, we can transfer Paul's ticket to your name."

Except this is a recipe for disaster. It takes me a second to realize what she's suggesting, but before I can say anything else, she's already sent a text to the other vet at my clinic. Her fingers are flying furiously over the screen of my phone. "Alec has you covered this week. You can go with me to Bora Bora. Don't say no. Just say 'Okay, Bay, let's go back to my place and pack.'"

Stunned, I repeat back what she just said and head out to my own little slice of heaven.

An hour later, Evan, my sister, is pulling up in my driveway with Bayleigh's honeymoon bag and cell phone. "'Bout time you two are taking this honeymoon together," she says. "Or should I call it a weddingmoon?"

Bayleigh and I both look at her, confused. "What?" I ask.

"You know, the vacation before the wedding, kinda like a babymoon, but... oh never mind." She waves us off, because we're both puzzled and laughing at her.

"Sure…" I drawl.

Bayleigh looks at me with wide eyes, shakes her head, and mouths, "Your sister is crazy."

I mouth back, "I know," before turning to my wild sister. "Hey, do you mind taking care of Lily and Daphne for a few days?"

"Of course not. I love those little wieners," she says as she picks up Lily so she can lick her face while Daph is barking at her feet.

"You can take them to the clinic during the day if you're going to work late. The techs love them." And they do. One day, Daphne conned those poor girls out of fourteen dog treats. Of course, she came home and shit them out all over my closet, so it was the gift that kept giving.

"Who wouldn't love a chubby, brown, hairy wiener?" she prompts with a laugh. I roll my eyes. The wiener jokes are never ending around here.

"Gross," Bayleigh says.

"Don't worry, big bro. I've got everything under control around here. Now, you two go enjoy Bora Bora."

"All right," I say and kiss her on the cheek. "Tell Mom and Dad I said bye and I'll see them in a week." She nods as I turn to Bayleigh. "You ready?"

"Let's do this."

We've both gone to the bathroom and in true road-trip-with-Bayleigh fashion, she loads the vehicle—a much more practical Dodge pickup—down with drinks and snacks for the drive to the hotel near the airport in Dallas. Our flight is at the ass-crack of dawn, plus she already had reservations.

When we hit the interstate, Bayleigh turns on one of our old road trip playlists, and we jam out to '90s and early-2000s hits the entire way… until we hit stupid Dallas traffic. Bayleigh knows me enough to know the music needs to be turned down while I navigate through this mess. I much prefer the lack of traffic in Sunnyville to this shit. I've always been happy in our small town and never felt a calling outside the town limits other than when I was away at school.

"I can't believe we're doing this," Bay breaks the silence when we're stuck in bumper-to-bumper traffic, and I nod in agreement. It is kind of crazy. What the fuck was I thinking going on vacation with her?

"I know; it's crazy." I pause. "Actually, it's a very *you* thing to do."

Bayleigh shrugs. "It kinda is, isn't it?" She chuckles. She's a lot like my sister, Evan, in her free-spirited ways, but not as crazy. Nor is she a ball crusher. No wonder they've always gotten along so well.

There's always been an easy camaraderie between us, and I can't believe that I almost lost it. I know that if she'd have married that jerk, I'd slowly lose her, piece by piece until there was nothing left of her.

"So, Bora Bora?" I ask, knowing it doesn't really seem like the type of place she'd pick. She's more of a cabin in the mountains kind of girl—or at least she was before she became somewhat of a celebrity. Maybe Hollywood changed her? I look over at her and wonder how much of the old Bayleigh is still hiding under the glitz and glamour. I guess I have a little over a week to figure it out.

"Yeah, wasn't my first choice, but Paul wanted to go somewhere tropical. I had the money, so I booked one of those huts over the water. There's hiking, fishing, and kayaking. I booked a couple of excursions Paul wouldn't bitch about, but I bet we can switch them out for some fun ones." She twirls her hair. "Oooh, maybe we can go snorkeling," she says excitedly.

I haven't been snorkeling since a spring break trip my senior year of college. I guess I haven't taken much time off to have fun since I started working for my dad.

"That sounds fun," I reply, matching her excitement as the traffic starts to move again. I have to remind myself that she's never been somewhere like this before.

She continues reading off the list of excursions she has on her phone as we pull up to the hotel we're in for the night.

Once we're checked in and we make our way to the room, the air has changed between us. It's strange, it's off, and it's… awkward as hell.

"Everything okay?" I ask.

"Yeah... well, no," she says hesitantly. "So I booked a king room and tried to get them to change it, but they're booked solid for the night. We're going to have to share a bed."

I laugh. That's it? That's the big deal that has her so worked up? It's a non-issue. I would never do anything to upset her or make her uncomfortable.

"What?" she asks.

"How many times have we shared a bed?" I prompt.

"Many," she replies, remembering all the times we would fall asleep in my bed in high school watching a movie. We've always been just friends, nothing more. That hasn't changed.

"So, no big deal. We'll just watch one of the movies on TV, and it will be no different," I lie to myself and to her. Something has already shifted between us. I just can't put my finger on it.

We order pizza and chat about what excursions we want to add to our trip, and she tells me about what the suite should look like when we get there. She's so happy and carefree. I love seeing her like this.

FOUR

LIGHT AS A FEATHER

Bayleigh

O h fucking shit. What do I do?

My eyes popped open the second the strong hand landed on my breast. I barely slept a wink the entire night. I tossed and turned this way and that while staying as close to the edge as I possibly could in fear that I would touch him in some way, because that would be weird. Yesterday afternoon, I was supposed to marry someone else, and now I'm in bed with another man. What does that even say about me? I'm not entirely sure I want to know.

Granted, the new man is Archer and we've known each other practically our entire lives. He's my best friend. Our entire childhood, I slept in beds with him and Evan. Our parents would put us down after a dinner party, and we would laugh and giggle and spy on our parents and definitely not sleep while they all hung out, drank wine, talked, and laughed.

More times than I can remember, we would finally drift off to sleep in a big bed, lined up like little soldiers with Evan somewhere in the mix. But this time feels different. This time is *definitely* different—mainly because he's curled up behind me, spooning me, and his hand is on my boob.

I was nervous and terrified to let him see how scared I was to be in this strange situation. That's weird, right? We've known each other our entire lives. But when we got to the hotel, after pizza and a movie, I remembered I was packed for a wedding night, not rooming with my childhood bestie who happens to be a hot guy. I could have crapped my panties when I opened my bag and saw the only items packed were scraps of lace and boxes of condoms.

What was I thinking?

I know what I was thinking. I was thinking my fiancé and I hadn't had sex in a really long time, and I was going to get laid in Bora Bora—and a lot, if the amount of lingerie I packed had anything to say about it. God, I was *so* naïve.

How could I not see it wasn't late hours at his office keeping him away from me, but Nurse Amy's vagina instead? And I had thought marriage and a steamy honeymoon would solve all our problems.

Tears sting my eyes—not for the loss of Paul, because I know in my heart of hearts that he wasn't for me. I didn't love him, not really. But I miss the loss of a partner. Someone to come home to and share my days and nights with. Someone who would be my future. Now, I'm all alone.

"What's the hold up?" Asher asked last night, and I had been too stunned to say anything, so I just stood there, knowing I needed to close the bag, light it on fire, and toss it out the nearest window.

But I didn't.

And holy hell, I should have, but in my defense, I was stunned, shocked, freaking frozen, and all of this left me stupid. There was a weird sexual undercurrent snapping about the hotel room, and I was distracted. So when I opened the suitcase and saw all the slutty panties and see-through nighties, I panicked. Like I said, there was a series of right choices involving fire and windows, and I did not choose right. To be fair, I didn't choose wrong either. I did bad. I did not do one damn thing. I should have, but I didn't. *My bad.*

Unfortunately, while I was not taking that time to run screaming from the room, Archer walked up behind me, took one look into my luggage, and then *audibly* swallowed.

I wasn't sure what he was going to do. It could have

been anything. For a second, I wondered if *he* was going to light it on fire and throw it out the window. It was a good move; someone should have done it. Instead, he just reached around me and flipped it closed, before turning to me and saying, "I think I saw a Target across the parking lot."

"Solid plan," I mumbled, and then we walked to the Target.

I grabbed a cart and just started dumping stuff in it. I was like a deranged *Supermarket Sweep* contestant, and there was no stopping me. Packs of granny panties? *Check.* A couple of plain beige bras? *Check-check.* We grabbed a few more of the basics and headed to the checkout counter where Archer put three bags of gummy bears on the counter and a bottle of wine.

I let out a huge sigh of relief. "Thank you."

"I got your back, Bay." And he did—he always did. I needed to remember that. I had nothing to be afraid of. Whatever was going on between us, it would just… go away, and we would go back to being the Bay and Arch we always were.

He scooped up my bags and carried them back across the parking lot for me. When he let us back into the room, I dug through them, looking for the one thing I forgot to buy in my mad dash—a fucking pair of pajamas.

"Fuck me," I mumbled, and Archer choked.

"What was that?" he asked after he cleared his

throat.

"I didn't get pajamas," I admitted.

"Hmm," he hummed absentmindedly, and then it dawned on him what I was saying. "Oh!"

"Oh."

And then he shocked the shit out of me by whipping his T-shirt over his head and handing it to me. "That should work."

"Uhh… yeah," I said before making my way to the bathroom to change.

We spent the rest of the night drinking wine and eating the leftover pizza and gummy bears, save for one bag he tucked into my carry-on for the flight. It was a great night with a great friend, but then it was time to go to bed, and I was as nervous as a Nebraska virgin on prom night.

We took turns brushing our teeth, climbed into bed, turned out the lights, and shut off the TV. I laid down on my side of the bed, and my body felt stiff as a board. Oh my gosh, what was I doing? I had no earthly idea.

I clung to the edge of the mattress. I was afraid of what would happen if our bodies touched. I couldn't let it happen, no matter what. I didn't know why; I just knew I couldn't. And I was right to worry, because the second Archer drifted off to sleep, he chased me across the bed and back.

Apparently, my bestie is now a cuddler.

At some point in the middle of the night, he pinned

me to the mattress, his heavy frame half draped over my back, and I'll die before I ever admit that the heat of his body combined with the heavy weight of his bulk was comforting as hell.

But I still didn't sleep. Instead, I felt guilty over how much I liked cuddling with him when I had an angry ex-fiancé at another location. What kind of hussy am I anyway? I do not want to answer that.

I swear my eyes had just drifted closed when his heavy palm crept up his borrowed shirt and covered my bare breast. His hand now scorches my skin where he touches me, and I hold my breath. I'm equal parts tit-illated and terrified. And it will also be a cold day in hell before I admit that one. I need to move. Maybe I can slide his hand off my body. I place my hand on his wrist and put pressure to slide him away, but instead, he growls a little, and his grip tightens.

Fuck me, that was not the plan, man. I repeat, that was not the plan! My nipple hardens, and I feel tingly in other places that should not be noted either. Shit, shit, shit. This is not good.

Maybe I can shimmy my body down the bed and get away. I pull in a deep breath and cock a hip to try to wiggle away, and when I do, I come into contact with something very long and very hard, and I know he doesn't sleep with his baseball bat anymore, so…. *No!* I'm not going to think about that.

I need to think about getting out of this bed before

the alarm goes off. *Think Bayleigh, think!*

And then it happens.

I hear the telltale click of the bedside clock radio click over, and the alarm beep-beeps over and over again. It's too late. I'm trapped like a rat. But this time, not wanting to be caught with my hand in the cookie jar—or with Archer's hand on my booby—I jump up and dive off the bed like an Olympian. Unfortunately, Archer was more tangled in my shirt than I realized, and he takes the hard fall with me, landing on top of me seconds after I hit the floor.

"Ouch."

"Fuck," he bites out. "Bayleigh?"

"Uhh… hi?"

"What happened?" he asks.

"I'm uhh… am just excited to get started on our trip," I lie lamely. "You sleep. I'll hit the shower first."

And then I jump up off the floor and race into the bathroom, leaving my clothes behind.

Well, there's no going back now.

Now, I'm committed… I think.

Right?

FIVE

STIFF AS A BOARD... LITERALLY

Archer

Waking up with my hand on Bayleigh's breast is not a horrible way to start my day.

Wait. Yes, yes it is. I cannot be thinking about my best friend that way.

I smack my forehead, willing the images of her in my T-shirt to go away. The worn cotton that's been washed just enough that it was almost translucent. The way it hit her just at her hip, still allowing me to see just a slight peek of her panties. White, plain, but with a broad lace trim around her hips sending the majority of the blood in my body straight to my dick. When it takes on a pulse of its own, I know I have to do something to stop this madness.

When we laid in bed last night, awkwardly trying not to touch each other, it was all I could picture. I've never been a snuggler before, but dammit, my body just gravitated toward her. Which led to Boobgate. What the hell was I thinking? I wasn't thinking—that's the problem. I was asleep, and clearly my hand had a mind of its own.

Now, she's in the shower, and I've got the worst case of morning wood ever. It's going to be a long week. Maybe I shouldn't go. But I can't let her go by herself either. She's hurt and vulnerable right now, and no matter how much I may want her, I need to protect her more.

I grip the base of my dick to try to get it to go down. My impulse is to lie here and stroke it until I come. My body needs the release more than it should, but I can't do that. I can't jerk off thinking of my hot best friend while she's in the adjoining room. I force myself to picture old women and puppies, baseball stats, and anything else I know that doesn't turn me on, and thankfully it works. And just in time too, as Bay walks out of the bathroom, wrapped up in a shitty hotel towel that doesn't seem to want to stay closed. She flashes me bits of leg here and there and I think I might have a heart attack. I'm too young to have a heart attack, right?

"It's all yours," she says, unable to make eye contact. She quickly moves over to her suitcase and roots around in it, pulling out jeans and a tank. There's a pale-pink blush staining her cheeks, and it's a teasing hint at what she might be like when she's turned on.

Was she as aroused as I was sleeping next to her?

Shit. I shouldn't think about her being turned on.

But I want to see if the blush on her cheeks stains the rest of her body all the way down. Are her nipples the same light-pink that teased me through the worn material of my T-shirt this morning?

I have to stop this. It's not right.

"Ahh... okay." I get up, grab my clothes from my bag, and make my way to the shower as quickly as possible.

I really need to release some tension before we fly to LAX to get on the overnight flight to Bora Bora. I couldn't jerk off in the bed we shared, but if I'm going to make it through the flight, I have to do something to relieve this tension.

I wrap my fist around my cock and begin to stroke, doing my best to imagine anything but Bayleigh, but she's literally all I can think about.

That pink blush on her cheeks and what it might look like on other places.

The lace of her panties peeking out.

The feel of her full breast, heavy in the palm of my hand.

All the other places on her body I want to see and touch and taste. Are her mouth and pussy as sweet as she is?

When I finally come, it just doesn't feel like enough. I want to fuck my best friend. It also makes me feel kind of gross. I've never really let myself think of Bayleigh like that until last night. I've loved her always, but she was also always out of reach in one way or another, so I never really allowed myself to imagine being with her in that way before. Waking up with her in my arms like that must have shaken some things loose, but I have to stuff those thoughts and feelings back in the fucking box they popped out of like a jack-in-the-box from sexy time hell, or else I'll never get our relationship back on track. Friendship. It's a friendship, not a relationship. We're friends. *Just friends.*

Shaking off the feeling, I hop out of the shower and dry myself off before putting my clothes on and heading back into the room.

Bayleigh is putting on her makeup when I round the corner. "What time do we need to be at the airport?"

"In about forty-five minutes. We need to leave in ten." She's methodical, mostly focusing on what she's doing and trying to avoid eye contact with me. I've embarrassed her, and I hate that. Bay should always feel comfortable with me. *Always.*

"Cool. Do you want to stop and grab something on the way, or eat at the airport?" I ask as I'm scratching my head. "I'm starving, and I need coffee bad."

"Gah, me too," she says, packing up her makeup

bag. I guess she's finished. Not that she needed much anyway. She's always been a natural beauty in that girl-next-door kind of way. "Let's grab a coffee there once we get through security though. If I drink something on the way, I'll inevitably need to pee while waiting in the security line."

"Sounds good." I begin packing up what I took out of my overnight bag and piling our stuff by the door so it's ready to go when she is.

Bayleigh clicks her tongue, looking around the room. "Got your passport and driver's license?" she asks as she feels under the bed and opens all the dresser drawers. What the hell could she be looking for? She makes her way into the bathroom, and I can hear her digging around in there too.

"Yes, I've got both," I answer her when she pops back out of the bathroom. I like things easy, but a little disorganization never hurt anyone. Bayleigh, on the other hand, is a bit of a nut in the way she needs things to be ordered. Hell, she even turns all the condiments in her fridge to face the same way. And she orders them by how much she likes them.

"Perfect," she says as she gets down on her hands and knees and looks under the bed and then wanders back into the bathroom to look one more time. I'm sure we didn't forget anything. We didn't even unpack any-thing really. Finally, she comes back out and makes her way toward me. "Ready?"

"Ready!"

"Bora Bora, here we come!" She fist-pumps the air like things weren't super awkward just a bit ago, so I go with it.

"Hell yeah, let's do this."

"Ladies and gentlemen, we're now arriving at Fa'a'ā International Airport. It's a beautiful, sunny day today. Roughly twenty-nine degrees—eighty-five degrees Fahrenheit for our Americans on board. We hope you enjoyed your flight. Thank you for flying Polynesian Airlines." The pilot gives us our information for the next flight to Bora Bora, since most passengers on board are headed in that direction.

"Oh my gosh, I can't believe we're finally almost there." Bayleigh looks out the window, sees the beautiful blue water, and realizes the airport landing strip is almost its own island. "Archer, we're going to be able to stop before the runway runs out, right?"

I laugh. "Yes, Bay. These pilots know how to land and stop a plane on this runway just fine."

She visibly tenses when the landing gear starts coming out right before we hit the ground with a thud. Not the easiest landing I've ever experienced, but not the worst either.

Our next flight is a quick hop compared to the last one, and before we realize it, we're being ushered via boat to our resort and then to our overwater villa.

"Holy cats, that water is so clear," Bayleigh says, looking down at the ocean right off the pier we're walking on. She's right. It looks like you can see all the way down to the bottom here. The water is a clear, tranquil blue. Fish flit and swim all around. This place feels almost… *magical.*

"The resort restaurants and exercise facilities are in the main part of the resort. And of course, there's a community pool with a fully stocked bar, but you do have your own private pool to enjoy as well…"

As the resort guide continues telling us where all the amenities are, I stare at Bayleigh. She's bright-eyed and so excited, practically bouncing on the balls of her feet like a human Tigger. And beautiful. She's so fucking beautiful. God, Paul is such a jackass. He had all of this at his fingertips, and he threw it away to bang his secretary. If Bayleigh were mine, I'd do everything I could to keep that excited smile on her face every day.

But Bayleigh's not mine. And why does the reminder of that tighten something in my chest?

I thank the bellhop and tip him, even though it is not customary in Tahiti. I can't not do it. It's ingrained in me.

The villa is not huge, but it's also not tiny by any means. The bedroom is completely open to the water and the pool deck with the white curtains blowing in the wind. But then it dawns on me. *One bed.* Casually, I scan the room. There's something else in here, right? Like a cot in the closet? Something, anything.

Bueller, help me out here. But alas, there is only one fucking bed. "Fucking" not being the operative word here. There is only one bed in this whole villa, which is basically one giant room.

I look around, seeing a sofa that does not look comfortable to sleep on for ten nights, but I may have to. Ten nights with Bayleigh, in the same bed. Nope. Can't. Ain't going to happen. Fuck me running. This is going to kill me. If I make it through this week and a half, I deserve a goddamn medal.

What's eleven days?

Ten nights?

That's practically nothing. I can do this. I will do this.

I'm so fucked.

I make a mental note to make an appointment with my chiropractor the second we land back in America. The sofa isn't even a whole sofa. It's like an oversized armchair at best. I'm not a giant, but I am pretty tall, and trying to fold up on that is going to hurt like a mother-fucker.

"Archer, come look at this." Bayleigh pulls me out of my thoughts. When I find her, she's standing out on the open deck, looking at the ocean and the pool. "Man, it's going to be a fun week and a half."

I nod like a freaking moron. "Uh-huh. Sure is."

A fun week and a half with a constant hard-on, because my best friend is fucking sexy as hell and I never noticed it before. And, of course, all the other lies I tell myself. *Follow me for more friendship advice. I'm clearly killing it here.*

"So what do you want to do first?" Bayleigh asks, looking at the resort amenities list. "It's almost lunchtime, and I just realized we skipped breakfast on the flight, so how about we go eat at the grill?"

"Sounds good to me. You know the way to make a guy happy is by feeding him, right?" I joke.

Really, I need any distraction right now, other than the bed that feels like it grows smaller by the minute. The focal point of the room is quickly becoming a major source of anxiety for me. My skin feels itchy, and I'm tempted to try to claw my way out of this room if need be. That would be weird if I ran screaming from the suite, right?

"Riiight," she jokes back, giving me a knowing smile. "I'm sure that's all it takes."

We both laugh at her sexually laced joke and begin walking to the main part of the resort. She wasn't hinting, right? I try to remind myself with every step that she is not for me; now isn't a good time for either of us.

Just friends. Just friends. Just friends.

Maybe if I keep repeating it over and over, I will

eventually believe it. Because right now, I don't want to. I want to take her in my arms and make her mine, timing be damned. I feel a little like the guy in *Shawshank Redemption* walking toward the electric chair. There's no way I'm going to survive this. Or was it *The Green Mile*? The fuck if I know; all I know is that I'm goddamned doomed.

We make our way up to the restaurant, admiring the beautiful island foliage and the interesting mountains off in the distance. By the time we get there, my heart is racing and I'm sweating a little bit more than I should. I'm in shape—I run and lift weights regularly to keep up with the animals I work with—but I feel a little like I'm about to have a heart attack, and I'm pretty sure it has everything to do with the woman walking beside me.

The grill is an outdoor open dining area with beautiful white-and-blue decorations overlooking the backside of the resort with the perfect view of the boats coming in and out for their excursions.

We're seated in one of the round sofa booths, and the hostess puts the menus super close together, assuming we're going to snuggle while we eat. Bay, always polite, scoots in toward the one in the middle, but once she leaves, she scoots a little farther over so we're sitting across from each other.

"It's so gorgeous here," she says, eyeing the open waters some more while tucking her hair behind her ear.

What I wouldn't give to be the one tucking it for her and kissing her neck.

Goddammit, stop thinking about kissing your best friend, Archer.

"It really is," I reply as I pick up my menu to distract myself. "What are you getting to eat?"

"Umm... I kinda want a pizza, but I don't think I can eat it all by myself, and since our room doesn't have a refrigerator…." She continues scanning the menu for something else.

"Pizza sounds good. I'm personally eyeing the margherita one."

She laughs. "Me too! Let's go with the margherita then."

"Sounds good."

Just as we set down our menus, the waiter takes our drink and food orders, and we sit in awkward silence for just a few minutes, before I decide to ask, "Bay, so now that you've had a little bit of time to process everything, how are you feeling?"

She looks at me, confused. "What do you mean?"

"About being a runaway bride." I laugh awkwardly and rub the back of my neck. "I mean, it was like that movie, you know?"

"Oh that." She takes a deep breath. "Well, I feel like I was a dumbass for going through with that wedding in the first place. Now that I think about it, something wasn't really right with Paul for a long time, and I just wanted the fairy tale so badly that I ignored all the signs."

I shrug. "You didn't know, Bay."

She shakes her head, then continues, "I mean, his cheating was literally right in front of my face. I was just so caught up in being a pretty-pretty princess for a day that I didn't see it. I didn't *want* to see it."

"Listen, we're all human, and you can't beat yourself up over that."

"I know. I just hate that my parents spent all that money for it to fall apart." She puts her head in her hands, choking back tears.

"Sorry, I didn't mean to make you upset." I reach over and rub her back.

"No, don't apologize. I need to face the facts sooner or later." She shrugs one shoulder. "Might as well do it now." I leave my hand on her back as she continues. "I was just so stupid, you know."

No, you weren't, I say to myself, because I don't want to interrupt her.

"Looking back, I knew for months that he was cheating. Late nights at the office. Random weekend *business* trips. I just never wanted to admit it to myself." She pauses and takes a deep breath. "My filming schedule was also crazy, so who knows how much more I actually missed. Especially those months I was having to spend a lot of time in Canada filming scenes. And the days leading up to our wedding, when I was filming things for the promotional tour."

"Bayleigh—" I start, before we're interrupted by our waiter who is back with our drinks, and perfect timing too, because Bayleigh ordered some fruity cocktail that looks to have plenty of alcohol in it. I ordered a soda, because I can't get drunk around her and risk crossing any lines. Especially with her being so vulnerable right now.

"Anyway, I kinda want to stop talking about it." She takes a huge sip. "Damn, this is one hell of a drink. You can tell there's a ton of alcohol in here, but you can hardly taste it. This is dangerous. Try it." She shoves the straw in my face, and I take a sip.

"Oh yeah, that is a dangerous drink." But I think she needs it. I would too if I had just left my fiancé at the altar after finding out I wasn't the only one in their life. She's been through a helluva time.

After lunch, we decide to spend time in our private pool. Bayleigh didn't plan any excursions today, since it was partially a travel day and, with the four-hour time difference, figured it would just be a lazy day, and I'm thankful for that.

I'm already in the pool when she walks out in her tiny yellow bikini that is leaving very little to the imagination. That old song keeps skipping and repeating through my head while I watch her, she walks to the edge of the pool and dives in.

"How's the water feel?" she asks, dipping her toe in.

"Perfect," I reply, grabbing her foot and pulling her into the water. She screams as she flies through the air, and her voice cuts off when she breaks through the surface.

"Stop! Archer!" She laughs when she comes up, completely soaking wet. "Why'd you do that?" She slaps my chest, and I laugh, pulling her in for a hug. We've always been cuddly with one another. I've never thought too much about it, but now, I know for certain that it was a…

Dumb idea.

I can feel her nipples poking through her suit and pressing against my chest. It sends a pulse straight to my dick. The water here is warm and does nothing to cool my desire for her. If she stays in my arms much longer, something long and hard and full of semen is going to pop up, and I do *not* mean a submarine.

I let go and splash her again, and she splashes back.

"Okay, okay!" She holds up her hands in surrender. "You win."

I stop and make my way over to the underwater ledge to sit down, admiring the most breathtaking view—Bayleigh, as she admires the second most beautiful view.

She turns her head, looking at me from over her shoulder when she senses me staring. "It's beautiful, isn't it?"

"Sure is," I answer honestly. *Sure is.*

SIX

BUTTERFLIES AND BATS AND THE WHOLE FREAKING BELFRY

Bayleigh

I feel a tingle go up the back of my neck as I lean against the edge of the illusion pool in our villa.

The glass sides of the pool make it seem like you could just… float away into the sea with nothing stopping you. The ocean is such a bright aqua that seems unreal, and the sherbet-colored sky of Tahiti paints a gorgeous picture, one I'm sure I'll never see anything like again in my life.

My skin feels tight from being in the sun all afternoon, but that's not what is grabbing my attention. I turn my head and look over my shoulder to see Archer watching me. My lips part, and I gasp. There's something about the way he's looking at me. It's different than any way he's ever looked at me before. Maybe it's the intent way he watches or the unbanked heat in his eyes, I don't know, but it sends a shiver up my spine.

I say something—it's stupid, I'm sure—but I'm not even aware of what the words are as they come out of my mouth. Whatever it was, he's agreeing with me, but I can't for the life of me focus on what is being said.

Junior high and high school were miserable for me. Not because I didn't have friends or belong to clubs. I was good at sports and in the drama club. Archer and I had loads of friends, including his sister, Evan. I was happy, but I was also quietly miserable, because I was in love with my best friend, and he dated anything with girl parts. That is, except for me.

College was worse. It was like he had something to prove, and he fucked his way through anything that breathed. Again, that was a demographic I was excluded from. It was almost a relief when I left college to move to L.A. I missed him, and I was devastated to leave him, but I couldn't take it anymore. It was like my life was suspended, waiting for him to notice me, while he was happily living his life.

So I moved on.

I dated, and I did it frequently. Leaving Texas freed me. I needed to get out from under the bubble that kept me stuck in one place as a front-seat witness to his sexcapades.

And then I met Paul, and everything seemed great. That is until I saw his secretary's text messages on his phone. But if I'm being totally honest with myself, I was having doubts before the incriminating text messages. I always knew something wasn't right. Paul isn't a bad guy, cheating aside, but he isn't Archer either. Not to mention the fact that I wasn't overly broken up about his infidelities was probably more than a red flag; it was the whole ticker tape parade.

But Archer has never looked at me like this. This look makes my nipples tingle and my pussy clench. My heart pounds in my chest, and my breath comes out in quiet, little pants. This is the look I waited years for him to send my way, only to feel sad or unwanted when, ultimately, he never did.

But this look sends butterflies through my belly. Butterflies that are as big as bats. And it makes me want to… hope. Those bat-sized butterflies must inhabit my belfry, because surely after twenty-five years of friendship, of watching him look at everyone that way but me, I would have to be crazy to even begin to hope, right?

And then he blinks and it's gone. Gone before I can swim across the pool to him. Gone before I can press my body against his and feel my soft places against his hard ones. Gone before I can beg him to kiss me, to make love to me. It's just gone… as if it was never there at all.

I sigh and turn back to the sunset. It's beautiful and romantic and, goddammit, it made me hope.

I'm glad he can't see my face as I blink back the few tears that surprised even me. I don't want Archer to know I've felt anything for him at all. I've avoided that awkward conversation for a quarter of a century, and I'd like to keep that going. It would break my heart to have to confess to him that I've been in love with him my entire life, only to have him tell me that he feels nothing at all. To see the pity in his eyes as he realizes we can't be friends anymore, because one day, he'll meet a great gal, fall in love, get married, and make beautiful babies. And if watching his parade of sorority girls in college was hard, that will devastate me.

I realize suddenly I've had enough of a walk down memory lane. I've had enough warm water and romantic sunsets. Now I need a little quiet and to be alone. I turn around and see… *something*. Something I can't identify flits over his stupidly handsome features before I swim toward the ladder.

"Where are you going?" he asks me.

"To shower," I answer with a false smile plastered on my face. "Give me about thirty and then the shower is all yours."

"Bay," Archer calls out, and I turn back to him again. "Yeah?"

"Are you all right?" His face softens, awash with concern for me and my emotionally battered state, and it breaks my freaking heart, because the one to batter it wasn't Paul, the cheating jackass. It was him.

"Yeah," I reply, rubbing my shoulder. "I think I just got too much sun. I need to shower off the chlorine and rub some lotion in."

"Ung," he gurgles, and it looks like he's swallowed his tongue. I replay what I just said and feel my face burn with embarrassment.

"Uhh…" I mumble. "I'm gonna go shower now. Like I said, it's yours in about thirty."

"Okay," Archer replies, and I roll my eyes at the sound of his poorly concealed laughter.

I haul myself up the ladder and out of the pool and grab my towel from the deck, quickly wiping the water droplets from my overheated skin. I sling the soft material around my body. If only it were an invisibility cape, then he wouldn't be able to see my less than graceful run into the villa.

In fact, I run like a chickenshit all the way into the bathroom and shut the door. I lean against the painted wood panel and wonder what the hell happened to my cool. I used to be such a cool chick, and now one painted sky and some sexy looks later, and I'm no better than an idiot.

"Fuck me," I mutter and drop the towel.

I reach into the shower and twist on the taps. The small room instantly begins to fill with steam from the flowing hot water. I pull off my yellow bikini, the most modest of my honeymoon attire. When I shopped for this trip, I imagined having my brains fucked out by my new husband and wanted to inspire those scenarios as much as possible. Now, it's a bit daunting.

Maybe I'll just wear the same one over and over again.

Maybe they have a gift shop. I wish I would've grabbed one at Target.

I let the scraps of material fall to the tile floor, and I step into the shower. The hot water stings my skin, making my lie of too much sun hold a modicum of truth. A painful price to pay for seeking the quiet I needed to cool off from Archer's heated looks and hungry eyes.

I pour shampoo in my hands and lather up my hair, dipping my head back underneath the spray. Did I imagine the way he looked at me? The wanting that burned in his eyes? Is the romantic locale playing tricks on my mind?

I upend my shower gel bottle onto a loofa and scrub my body. The scrape of the coarse sponge brings my nerve endings to life. I gasp when the loops brush over my hard nipples and arch into the feel of them in my own hands.

Could I? Should I?

I imagine the way Archer looked at me, but this time, he swims to me, pressing his hard body behind mine and holding me in his arms. He would kiss the side of my neck where it meets my shoulder in that sensitive place that drives me wild. I would tip my head back on his strong shoulder and take all that he was willing to give me.

"Ohh, Archer," I would moan when he slid his hand down the front of my bikini bottoms to find me warm and wet, and it would have not one thing to do with the heated pool.

As I picture his hand on my most private place, bringing me the pleasure I know he never will, I gently trail my own hand down my belly and over my bare mound to stop between my thighs. Maybe I'll be able to bear being so close to him after I've had an orgasm or two, even if they are a solo show.

SEVEN

Archer

ittle flickers of light—that's all that's left of the day as I sit at the end of the pool, elbows on the edge, staring out at the now darkness, since the sun has set. You can see other villas in the distance over the water. *Just little flickers of light.*

I hope Bayleigh is okay. The tension between us was so thick it was palpable, like a real living thing between us. I'm having a hard time understanding why. One minute, we were laughing, and the next, things got super awkward. Maybe I shouldn't have pulled her in like I did. But it was funny, and she laughed. We used to play around like that all the time. I didn't think anything of it, but now I can't think of anything else.

It was the hug. I felt it. The sudden sexual tension—it's there, coating everything around us with a thrilling haze—and neither of us can fucking act on it. *Never.* Not in a million years. I won't risk our friendship. She's not just another woman in my life that I can fuck and discard like yesterday's furniture rental mailers. She's Bayleigh Hart. My best friend. My everything. And not one thing more than that, because she can't be.

I would never hit it and quit it with her. It's better this way, ignoring the sexual tension. We'll just go on as we always have and leave it at that.

It's been about thirty minutes, so I decide it's safe to jump out to shower myself. As I climb out, I grab one of the towels to dry off before walking into the villa. The bathroom is actually really huge. There's a bath and dressing area and two sinks behind the bed. To the right is the toilet, and to the left is where the huge rainfall shower is that I can't wait to jump in, but Bay is still in there.

I step into the toilet area to relieve myself before gathering my stuff so I can jump in quickly when she's out. Before I step back in the bedroom to give her some privacy to change, I hear a long moan and "Ohh, Archer."

Wait. What?

I stop dead in my tracks. Did I really just hear that? I mean… obviously not. Clearly, my sudden unrequited feelings for her and the pent-up sexual fantasies have caused me to lose the tenuous hold I had on my sanity.

Out of pure masculine instinct, I step toward the shower, and I hear, "Mmmmm, Ace. Don't stop."

Yeah, I definitely did not misunderstand that one. And her moaning the nickname she gave me years ago when we were just kids. This is a lot to process. But what do I do now?

Do I go in there? Do I ignore it and pretend like it never happened? Easier said than done when my cock is so hard it could drive nails right now. I run my palm down my face. If I thought I harbored sexual fantasies about my best friend before, that was nothing compared to the X-rated visions of her that are flitting behind my eyes.

Her on the edge of the pool, her long legs wrapped around my waist.

Her on her knees in front of me with her pretty pink lips wrapped around my cock.

In the shower, bent over as she braces herself against the tile wall while I take her from behind.

Shit. I can't keep doing this. I need to get out of here before she hits her grand finale, which—by the way her panting and moans have picked up in tempo—I'm thinking is soon. There's no way I could go in there. It would ruin me for all other women. It's better if I get out of here while I can. I rewrap the towel around my waist, shoving my delinquent dick down as best as I can, and step back outside to lay on one of the loungers until she's finished.

She'll avoid looking at me, her face probably a delicious pink. She'll know she thought of me while she touched herself, while she made herself come thinking of me. But she won't know that I know. Now, I'm plagued with the knowledge of what she sounds like when she's aroused, when she reaches for her orgasm, but not what she looks like when she takes it. What would she sound like if I kissed her all over, if I licked her pussy until she screamed?

Does her mouth make a pretty little *O*, or does she squeeze her eyes tight? I wonder if she'll be pink like that all over from the orgasm she's giving herself in my honor. But then again, that's not mine to have either.

I'm staring up at the stars in the sky when I hear Bayleigh clear her throat. "The shower is yours, Ace."

I flinch at the name, now knowing she just moaned it out in the shower. "Okay, thank you."

I make my way back into the bathroom area where I left my shower stuff on the counter and get under the stream of water. Remembering the walls are thinner than they seem, I opt out of relieving myself. As much as it sucks. Because now all I can picture is Bayleigh with her hand between her legs. I want to wrap myself around her and cover her hand with my larger one. I want her to show me how she likes to be touched, and then I want to take over. I want to make her come, make her beg and scream. Make her want to be mine. But I don't. I don't do any of that.

It takes everything in me not to grab my dick and rub one out, but that feels wrong with my conflicting emotions and piss-poor timing flinging around in my brain. I quickly scrub my hair and body to get the day's travel and pool chlorine off me.

When I step out, dry off, and am ready for bed, I see Bayleigh has turned on the TV to some cooking channel. "It was either this, the weather, or some sappy romance movie I'm not really in the mood for." She pipes up when she sees me staring at it.

"Cooking show it is." I lazily smile at her. Who can blame her for not wanting a romance movie? She just ended a long relationship. Sure, he was a douchebag, but she was going to marry him. That's bound to stir up some kind of emotions in her.

"I'll have you know that this is *Chef To Go* and I love him," she replies. "He accosts random bewildered looking people in the supermarkets and follows them home so that he can teach them to prepare an actual meal instead of frozen garbage that's full of chemicals."

"That sounds… appetizing."

"It's fantastic," she says as she becomes more and more excited explaining the show setup to me. "I met him once at an opening in Los Angeles. He's super nice and so is his girlfriend."

She had me going there for a second. A pang of jealousy hit me square in the gut that she knows this famous chef with the pretty face. But I don't have any excuse to be jealous. If she wanted to date him, there's nothing I could do to stop her. And I wouldn't either because I only every wanted her to be happy.

And if that's the honest truth, then why am I so relieved to hear that he's in a serious relationship and Bay loves his girlfriend.

I move to the closet and begin pulling out the extra blankets I saw in there earlier today when the resort guide was showing us around.

"What are you doing?"

"I'm sleeping on the sofa," I answer matter-of-factly. She can't possibly think we can sleep in the same bed after the night in the L.A. hotel and what just happened in the pool—then what I know she did in the shower. Not that she knows that I know what she did in the shower, because if she knew that I knew what she knows, Bay would lose her ever-loving shit. So it's best she doesn't know that I know.

"Uh, no. Ace, don't be dumb." She pulls back the covers on the opposite side of her and pats. "We're still adults, as far as I can tell. This bed is *huge*. I'm not letting you sleep on that tiny sofa. I'm also not sleeping on that tiny sofa," she adds.

"Fine," I say and put the extra blankets back in the closet but keep the two extra pillows with the intention of putting them between us. Maybe that will keep me from grabbing her breast in the middle of the night again.

Yeah, and maybe the Pope isn't Catholic after all.

When I slide under the covers, I realize just how thankful I am that I'm not sleeping on that fucking joke of a sofa. I'm not sure my back could take it. It's not that I'm old or in bad shape; I look pretty good, if I do say so myself. It's that it's fucking tiny, and I don't know how to fold my long frame up like an origami crane to fit.

"I haven't checked my phone all day, have you?" I ask.

"Nope." She pops the P. "And I really don't want to either."

"Me neither," I reply, and as I say the words out loud, I realize I really don't.

My dad is running the clinic, so I know everything is fine on that end, and there's a backup clinic about thirty miles from ours that we partner with when one of us gets overloaded or has a special case. Evan has my bitches under control, and they love her more than they love me, 'cause she spoils them with treats when really they should be on a diet. Dachshunds are notorious for being fat, lazy, stubborn assholes, but they're really the best dogs in the world. And other lies I tell myself, because those fat little sausages have me wrapped around their stubby little paws.

"Good, let's just agree to leave them off while we're here, shall we?" she asks, and I nod. I wouldn't want to deal with the aftermath of leaving a shitty groom at the altar either. He had been calling her nonstop for the first twenty-four hours; now, I don't know. What would I do if she went running back to him? I just don't know.

"Deal. Our families have the resort number and information; they can call if there's an emergency."

"Yup."

For the next little bit, we sit in semi-silence. The television is going as background noise, but neither of us are paying a lick of attention to it. I can't focus on anything but her. I didn't even notice we never made it to dinner.

Before long, I hear her breathing even out, and I reach over to grab the remote off her lap so I can turn it off and catch some sleep myself.

The next morning, I wake up to Bayleigh whispering my name. "Oh, good morning, sunshine!" she says a *lot* too excitedly for me.

"What time is it?" I ask.

"Seven-thirty." She clears her throat. "Our first excursion is at 9:00 a.m., so we need to get to breakfast pretty quickly. On the list today is breakfast at eight, then we're going on a jet ski tour that includes a snorkel cruise with stingrays and sharks, which I'm not overly excited about, but still... it's going to be a *blast*! When they bring us back, we'll have just enough time to shower and change for dinner. I made reservations at the resort steakhouse."

"Wow, you've got this whole day mapped out, huh?"

"Have you met me?" She laughs, and I laugh with her, because honestly, I expected nothing else. She's a planner through and through. "Today is one of our busier days. I changed stuff around yesterday on the flight, since you're more adventurous than Paul." She grimaces. "And today was the only day the jet ski people had left on their schedule."

I nod. "Sounds fun. Let's do this." I get dressed quickly, and we make our way up to the main part of the resort.

Once we're seated for breakfast with our plates filled from the buffet, I ask her about this excursion we're going on. I've been snorkeling before, and it's fun, but I'm not anywhere near expert level. And even though I love animals, I'm not gonna lie—the stingray and shark part scares the living bejesus out of me. But she's so excited about it, so I pretend like I'm not scared of being stung like Steve Irwin was. *May he rest in peace.*

"Well, it's for beginners or first-timers. Have you ever been?" she asks as she stuffs a forkful of scrambled eggs into her mouth.

"Once, and it's fun."

"Awesome, so when we're finished eating here, they'll pick us up in front of the hotel."

She describes how the whole day is going to go in detail, like she's studied the booking page a million times. And her excitement is everything I never knew I needed and now everything I want.

To put that smile on her face every day is a new goal of mine.

EIGHT

SCREAM LIKE A GIRL

Bayleigh

"I'm so excited!" I cheer as I bounce on the balls of my feet while we wait for our ride to the marina.

"I see that." Arch smiles at me indulgently. This is why I love him so much. I mean, I don't *love him*, love him. He's my best friend. He's known me practically my entire life. He gets me. Archer doesn't shame me or make me feel guilty for wanting or needing something different than he does.

I've never been snorkeling in open waters before, and the fish by the villa are so beautiful I cannot wait to see what's farther out. It's a little risky; I'm not that great of a swimmer. In fact, I can tread water at best. I wonder if he knows that. Sure, I spent all our time at the lake either on a boat or the shore, never waterskiing with the boys. He has to know, right? I guess we'll find out.

A rickety Toyota 4Runner from the '90s pulls up to the front of the resort. The paneling on the side facing us has been completely ripped off. It looks like someone either sideswiped him or he sideswiped someone else. I'm not sure I want to know. I don't think I want to be a witness. I feel like this is how you end up in a bathtub full of ice, missing something vital.

"Hey, bro," the driver calls out. "I'm Chris. Are you guys the Hart party?"

My first inclination is to say no. I would be lying if I said there wasn't a huge part of me that wanted to say no and then run like hell. But I'm also done with playing it safe. I'm done being afraid to live my life. I need an adventure, and dammit, I'm going to get one.

"That's us," I reply.

"Awesome possum," he says. "Climb aboard the starship."

Archer pulls open the rear passenger door for me, and it makes an awful groaning sound. I refuse to let it bother me. I just climb in the car with a smile on my face, and Archer slides in behind me.

"Why do I feel like I'm about to die?" he whispers in my ear.

"Don't be ridiculous." I roll my eyes. We're not going to die. We just need to live a little.

"I just need to make one quick stop on the way to the marina," Chris says cryptically.

We drive through the village, and I decide to take in the scenery. When will I ever get to see a place as beautiful as this again in my lifetime? I might not. Chris takes a turn off the main drag and winds his way through a rundown neighborhood. I'm starting to have my situational danger sirens ping in my head.

"Where are we going?" I ask casually, and Archer side-eyes me, the jerk.

"Oh, now someone's worried about personal safety?" he leans down into my space and says into my ear.

"Shh."

"Oh, I just need to place a quick bet on a cock fight," Chris says, and my eyes go wide. He parks the car in front of a sketchy house and runs inside.

"I'm pretty sure that's illegal here," Archer whispers in my ear.

"Uhh…" I start, but I don't have any words to fill in the gap.

"Now I know we really are about to die," Archer drawls.

"Shh!" I whisper-yell. "Let's just be real still, and maybe it'll be like we were never here."

"How often did that work for you when we were kids?"

"Almost never."

"That's what I thought."

I let out a frustrated sigh. I just want to live a little, go on an epic adventure, not die in some remote neighborhood of the village or go to jail in a foreign country.

"I'm sure it'll all be fine," Archer says, reading my mood.

Suddenly, the front door of the sketchy house flies open, and Chris comes running out. He jumps in the driver seat of the 4Runner that he never turned off and guns the engine, beads of sweat dripping down his forehead.

"Whew," Chris says to us, or maybe himself, as he wipes his brow with the back of his hand. I don't know, and it worries me. "That was a close one."

"Is it too late for me to amend that statement?" Archer asks me.

"Yes."

"I was afraid you'd say that."

"Just don't ask for clarification," I tell him out the corner of my mouth. I've gone with "the no sudden moves" plan of action.

Chris drives us to the marina, where he hands us off to the boat captain who is not happy he had to wait for us. His other two passengers this morning are professional scuba divers from Japan, and I can't help but wonder why they're on a snorkel tour for beginners.

"Cock fight?" the captain asks once Chris speeds

away. I just nod once. "I thought so."

He loads some pretty serious-looking tanks and other equipment onto the boat, and we follow him up, carrying our little tote bag of masks and snorkels.

"I thought this was a beginner trip," I say hesitantly as I look at all the diving gear.

"Oh, it is," he answers. "But I know all the best spots, so I'll drop them off and then take you guys to the cove."

It sounds innocent enough. What could possibly go wrong?

Thirty minutes later, as Archer and I float in the middle of the ocean all alone, I know exactly what could go wrong.

The boat captain did indeed know the best dive spots, and he drove the professional divers to the first one. They happily sat on the edge of the railing and leaned back, gracefully falling into the clear blue water with smiles on their faces. When they bobbed to the surface, they gave a jaunty wave and then sank below the water.

The boat captain waved and then motored away. I should have been alarmed then. I wasn't, but I should have been. They were professional divers. They could clearly take care of themselves. Archer and I needed adult supervision, even if the adult looked to be still a little drunk from the night before.

When he drove fifteen minutes to this spot where

we are now, the divers were nowhere in sight, and I was a little nervous.

"Here's your first spot," he told us, and we donned our fins and masks like fucking idiots. The sweet summer children we were in all our naïveté jumped off the boat and into the water. Well… Archer jumped; I more or less fell off the boat, but it was fine.

Everything was fine.

And then he left. I mean it. The boat captain waved to us and drove off. What the fuck? I figured he'd stay with us and then take us with him to go get the pros, not leave us floating in the middle of the ocean.

"What the fuck just happened?" Archer asks me as the boat disappears into the horizon.

"I-I have no idea."

"Did you know he was going to leave us?" he asks calmly.

"No," I answer. "I had no idea."

"I didn't get that impression either," he says. "He'll probably come back."

"I hope so."

"Let's just look at some fish and hope for the best," he murmurs. "If he's not back in an hour, I'll hit the panic button on my watch."

"Oh, okay," I agree, even though I shouldn't. I should want him to hit the panic button now.

We swim around and look at all the beautiful fish in the water. I've never seen anything like it before. When

Archer realizes I'm struggling to keep up with him, he gently takes me by the hand and tows me along with him, helping me keep up.

As luck would have it, a few minutes later, we see the boat coming back toward us. A sense of relief falls over me, knowing he didn't leave us out here as shark bait.

Once the boat captain gets closer to us and lets the anchor down, he hoists us back up on the boat and says, "You'll love the next site better."

Archer and I look at each other, both a little excited and terrified. Still hopeful we're not going to be shark bait. Unless this is just a game to the captain, giving us a sense of relief before killing us off.

The professional divers are nowhere in sight. He either killed them or forgot about them. Or he dropped them off at another dive site before picking us up. I'm hoping for the latter.

This time, he drives us to a beautiful cove. We can see the shore, but we're still a few miles away. We jump off the boat—again, Archer is as graceful as a cat, and I'm as graceful as an overweight walrus—and this time, we wave back as the boat captain drives away.

Archer takes my hand again, and I feel butterflies in my belly. Tropical fish flit this way and that, and the water is so clear. I kick my feet and chase the fish. I feel like a happy mermaid just living my best life in the warm water and sunshine.

And then I feel a tap on my shoulder. I look over to Archer, and he points down directly below us. I don't see anything, so I look back, and he frantically points down again. I blink my eyes to clear them, and then I see it. About twenty feet below us is the mother of all stingrays. Like the kind that could kill you if they weren't so docile. I don't feel like sticking around to find out.

A shrill scream is ripped from my lungs, and I try to jump out of the water, even though we're a few miles from the shore. I mean, just call me Jesus, because I walked on water. I was like those funny little *Jurassic Park* lizards you see on Discovery Channel with their tiny feet moving in fast circles to carry them across rivers. Never mind that the boat and captain are long gone, I don't care. I need away from the giant sewer cap of death.

"Bayleigh!" I hear Archer shout, but again, I don't care. "Seriously, Bay. Come back."

"Nooo!" I scream.

"Oh my God," he shouts. "Stop screaming."

"I can't!"

"You're such a girl," he gripes as he chases after me.

"That's because I am a girl!"

"Would you stop trying to get away from me," Archers growls as he grabs me from behind and pulls me back into him.

"I'm not trying to get away from you," I snap. "I'm

trying to get away from the happy little death machine."

"It's not going to hurt you."

"Tell that to Steve Irwin!" I shout, and he wrestles me down. When my head goes underwater for the fifth time and I come up spluttering, I think maybe he's trying to drown me. This is it. This is how I'm going to die. I feel like the *Twilight* intro.

And then the captain shows up and offers us a hand back onto the boat.

I have been rescued.

NINE

NETFLIX AND CHILL

Archer

The boat ride back to the resort is uneventful. Bayleigh is still calming down from her over-reaction of the stingrays, and it's taking everything in me to hold in a laugh, but I manage until we get back to our bungalow.

And that's when I can't hold it in any longer. I laugh so hard that my stomach muscles hurt.

"What's so funny?" Bayleigh side-eyes me.

"I can't believe you picked out the sketchiest snorkeling trip on this island!" I'm still laughing about it, but she's unimpressed. "Where did you find this one anyway?"

"Uhhh, right here," she says as she makes her way through the villa and into the bathroom. She comes back with one of those cheap acrylic frames with a flyer in it that clearly says *Beginners Snorkeling Experience. Best Rated on the Island.*

"Well, zero stars, do not recommend," I drawl.

And that's when Bayleigh starts laughing. It's just one little giggle at first, nothing more than a hiccup. And then another and another until she's laughing so hard tears stream down her face.

"You're such a dork," she says as she slaps my chest. I grab her hand instinctively, and we both just stand there for what seems like an eternity but in reality is just a few seconds. She pulls her hand back and says, "Uhh, I'm going to jump in the shower and get ready for dinner." Before I can reply, she turns around and starts walking away from me.

I don't know what that was, but I liked it way more than I should've. I'm tempted. More than I should be. Maybe it's the sun and the sand; maybe it's the romantic setting. But it's all starting to get to me.

TEN

BEST DAY EVER

Bayleigh

Amazing. That's the only word I can use to describe today. It was, simply put, amazing. I've never seen water so blue or fish so brightly colored—our potential tragic death in the ocean notwithstanding.

And Archer. There's just something about him today that's… I don't know, different. He's always been one of my best friends, but he's been more attentive, more protective than usual on this trip. Maybe it's the nature of how we got here, him running away from my doomed wedding day with me and all. But maybe, just maybe, it's not.

I stay lost in my thoughts, completely consumed with all things Archer, as I flip the taps in the shower on and get the water flowing. I strip out of my suit and toss it in the sink to rinse it out while the water heats up. When I'm done with my task, I pull my hair down from its binding and step under the spray. The water stings my skin as it washes away all the salt and sand.

I lather shampoo in my hair. I think I got a little too much sun today. I'm not burned, but it stings just a little. So does the knowledge that even though he's been protective and attentive, it doesn't mean anything. Archer has never loved me like I've loved him, and I don't see that changing anytime soon.

I turn off the taps and grab a towel, drying off quickly and pulling on leggings and a tank. I dry my hair and slather some moisturizer on my face, but I don't feel like getting all dolled up now. My heart's just not into it.

I bet I can talk Archer into staying in tonight. I think room service and Netflix is just what the doctor ordered for this particular ailment—a broken heart.

ELEVEN

WANNA GET DRUNK?

Archer

The next several days go by in the blink of an eye. We both want to stay busy, so we do a bike tour of the island and swim. I check parasailing off my bucket list while Bayleigh stays on the boat, because "No way am I going to fly behind a boat going fifty miles per hour." Her words. I just laughed and scheduled my time.

Tonight, our dinner is the traditional Polynesian experience.

I'm lounging out on the deck, waiting on Bay to finish getting dressed. We went to the shops this morning and bought clothes to wear for tonight. Me, a Hawaiian button-down shirt to wear with my khaki shorts and flip-flops, and Bayleigh, a palm-printed maxi dress. When she walks out, I'm speechless.

The dress is perfect on her. Tightly fitted in the right places with a slit that goes way too far up.

"How do I look?" she asks, twirling around. She's free and happy, and I'm thankful, because I know when we go back home in two days, the weight of the world will be on her shoulders again.

"Beautiful," I reply as I stand up and begin walking toward her. I jokingly reach my hand to her to help her down the steps. "My lady."

She giggles. It's the carefree sound I love, and she complies gladly. With her other hand, she grabs her dress to lift it up, since it drags slightly behind her. I don't know if it's supposed to do that or if she's just short, but it's cute nonetheless.

"Thank you, sir," she says, playing along with my chivalrous ways. I expect her to let go of my hand, but she doesn't. We walk hand in hand down the walkway until we get to the hut where dinner is.

We check in with the hostess, and she guides us to our table—front row where the fire pit is and where the dancers will eventually be dancing. She places the drink menu at the center of the table, then says, "Your waiter will be with you shortly to take your drink order. Enjoy."

We both tell her thank you and take turns looking at

the menu. I decide on a rum and Coke, and Bayleigh orders a fruity island drink, and says, "Keep 'em coming."

I laugh. "You plan on getting drunk tonight?"

She tucks her hair behind her ear and shakes her head. "No… I think I just want a few drinks."

"Same," I agree. I need to keep completely sober around her so I don't do anything I'll regret.

When we both have our plates full of the wonderful deliciousness from the buffet, we dig in. Bayleigh is almost a full drink in when she asks, "So tell me your funniest pet parent story."

I think for a second, because there have been many since I started working for my dad, but settle on one of my favorites. "Well, there's this lady—she's probably in her late sixties—who comes in with her parrot. No matter how many times we tell her we don't see exotic animals, she still comes in." I pause to take a sip of my drink. "We just roll with it now and call one of my dad's college buddies that specializes in parrots for treatment, but this parrot cusses, and it's the funniest thing. Especially living in the Bible belt."

"No way." She laughs. "I can only imagine how well that goes over."

"Yeah, well, you know my mom. She's never said a cuss word in her life and would slap me silly if I said one in front of her." She nods and waits for me to continue. "Well, this parrot comes in and starts calling everyone it sees a bitch."

Bayleigh nearly spits out her drink. "Oh. My. Gosh. No!"

"Oh yeah. So when she gets up to the front desk, which my mom was working that day, the bird says, 'fucking dumb cunt.'"

She's full-on laughing now, but quietly as to not make a scene with the other guests around us.

I take a sip as the waiter brings another drink for each of us, then continue. "So, yeah. You can imagine the look on my mom's face. Dad and I were right behind her, and we were having the hardest time holding in our laughter."

"I'll bet." She swipes a tear from her eye, because she was laughing so hard she's crying.

"So Mom got her checked in, then handed the front desk over to one of the techs until the lady was gone with her cussing parrot."

About that time, the dancers come out playing the drums, effectively ending the conversation there as we watch the traditional Polynesian show. And our waiter keeps the drinks coming. I really have no idea what's going on with the show though, because I cannot take my eyes off Bayleigh. I think in some way I've always loved her, but it wasn't until a few days ago that I began to see her as more than just a friend.

We finish the night off uneventfully going back to our bungalow and going to bed. Bayleigh just the right amount of drunk to make her sleepy.

Me, not near drunk enough, but that's for the best.

TWELVE

I'M A MERMAID!

Bayleigh

"Look at meee!" I shout as I bob up and down in the water around and under our villa. "I'm a mermaid!

"I see that." Archer laughs.

As soon as I jump up, I belly flop back down. I don't care. The water is so blue and sparkly. I've never seen anything like it before. It's cool against my heated skin. This morning, I decided I was going to jump into the water from the villa. I didn't want the safety of the pool today. No, I was going to live my life, and that's exactly what I did.

I'm no longer going to be encumbered by the negative thoughts and judgments of others. I spent way too long worried about what Paul would think of my antics and if he would be embarrassed or upset with me. But today, I realized, who the fuck cares? The only person I should be worried about what they think of me is me.

And today, I want to live my life. Today, I want to swim and play in the pretty blue water. I want to laugh and enjoy myself, and that's exactly what I set out to do. The world will be waiting when we get home, but for now, I just need a little fun in the sun.

I swim and splash and play. Archer never joins me. He opts instead to lie on one of the loungers and tan. But that's fine by me. New Bayleigh doesn't need others to tell her what she can and can't do. New Bayleigh is fine doing her own thing.

And I do until I'm plum tuckered out. I flop over to the edge of the little dock the villa sits on and rest my arms on the ledge.

"I'm tired," I announce with a huff.

"I see that," Archer says when he pushes his sunglasses to the top of his head and looks at me before tipping his head down to look at his watch. "Want to get changed and grab some dinner?"

"Yeah," I answer. "But pull me out first. This mermaid is pooped."

He chuckles, pushes up from the lounger, and walks over to the edge of the dock. Archer bends over and holds out a hand for me to take. When I place my hand in his, he hoists me out of the water with one arm like I'm the lightest thing in the world. The muscles and tendons in his forearm flex and pull, and I'm not gonna lie; it's sexy as hell.

"You wanna go first?" he asks me, breaking me free of my filthy thoughts about my best friend.

"Uhh… yeah," I answer, and then like a scared little rabbit, I race around him and right into the villa. I shower as quick as I can and feel the heat hit my face when I think about the past funny business I gave myself in this very shower, thinking of him.

I jump out, towel off, and pull on panties, a bra, and a soft cotton tank dress that hits just above my knees. It's a pretty lipstick-red that flows around my hips but clings in all the right places. It's not supposed to be sexy, but it kind of is in an understated way.

I should change.

I don't want him to think I dressed sexy for him. Even though I kind of did. Shit. What do I do now?

There's a knock on the bathroom door. "Everything all right in there?" Archer calls out.

"Uhh… yeah. I'm just about done in here," I reply, and I am, because I'm fucking busted. I can't change now. He'll know I did, but he won't know why. Shit!

I leave my hair down to dry in messy waves. The salt from the ocean is making my normal curls a little island-wild, and I like it. I leave the makeup off my face and let my tan shine on its own.

I push open the door and see him leaning against the wall opposite the door. "It's all yours."

"Thanks," he says as he saunters past me with a wink and his clothes wadded up in his hand. Jesus, I need to get it together. I'm a real mess right now.

Archer jumps in the shower to get ready for tonight. We're just going to keep it casual and eat at the bar and hang out by the pool.

That is, until the hotel phone rings. I assume it's the front desk calling about checkout tomorrow. "Hello."

"Hey, Bayleigh." It's my agent. It must be an emergency if she's calling me on this trip. Or she's calling because she couldn't wait another day for me to get home so she could yell at me about the PR nightmare I probably caused.

THIRTEEN

Archer

Once I'm out of the shower, I hear Bayleigh talking to someone, and upon further inspection, I see she's on the hotel phone.

"Yes... okay... I understand. That sounds awesome. What day should I get in? I don't know if I'll have a plus-one or not... okay... thank you." She hangs up and then startles when she realizes I'm in the room. "Sorry, my agent."

"Oh, okay. Is everything all right?" I ask awkwardly. After the moment we shared, I feel… off, not quite balanced right. I don't know how to get back to who we were before or how to move us forward.

"Yeah, the premiere of that movie is a week after we get back, so I'll need to go back to L.A. for that. Then it will be released in theaters next month." She shuffles from one foot to the other. Almost like she's nervous.

"That's awesome! Are you excited?"

"Of course! It's my first big role in a movie." She pauses and looks around like she's nervous.

"You okay?" I ask, moving toward her, because she doesn't seem excited. I want to hug her and make everything better.

"Yeah, it's just…" She reaches behind her and rubs the back of her neck, trying to get rid of the tension there. "News broke of the not-wedding."

"Oh shit."

"Yeah. And apparently Paul is doing a tell-all with one of the tabloids sometime this week." She walks back to the vanity to finish her makeup, but she just sits there staring at herself in the mirror, yet I get the feeling I'm the only one noticing her reflection.

I walk over and squat down so I'm below eye level. "Bay," I say quietly to get her attention, and she turns to look at me. "Is there anything I can do?"

"No," she breathes. "There's no stopping it now. I probably should've just cancelled this trip to deal with the fallout. I just…" I reach up to wipe a tear that's slipped out of her eye. "I just didn't think anything would come of it, since I'm still a nobody."

"You're not a nobody," I tell her. It feels empty like

a half-truth, because what I really want to tell her is, to me, she's everything. "You're Bayleigh *Fucking* Hart."

That at least got a laugh out of her.

"I don't really feel like doing anything tonight," she says, and I hate that she looks so despondent. "Can we just stay in tonight?"

"I love you, but no," I tell her.

"Thanks, you're the best— Wait, what?" she asks, and she's so fucking cute the way she thinks I'm just going to go along with whatever she wants, but I'm not that kind of friend. She should know that by now. What is she, new here?

"You need to get out and get over it," I answer. "Let's rip it off like a Band-Aid."

"Ugh," she says. "You're the worst."

"If by 'worst,' you mean totally fucking awesome, then yes."

"If by 'awesome,' you mean ridiculous," she replies with a smile.

"If by 'ridiculous,' you mean will buy you copious amounts of tequila to get you over your public shame and heartbreak, then yes."

"You had me at tequila," she says with her hand over her heart in a show of faux-seriousness. This is the Bayleigh I love so much. This is the woman I can be free to be myself with.

"I know."

She breathes out a sigh of relief. "That actually sounds really good." I stand up and finish getting dressed.

When I walk back out of the bathroom, I realize what she's wearing. A cute red dress. Tight. Showing just the right amount of curves to make her even sexier than usual but without even trying. Which just makes me fucking want her. Fuuuck. It's like the universe hates me, and I have to keep thinking of puppies and old ladies to keep my dick from giving away the fact that she turns me on. I can't be thinking of my best friend like that. *She's not for me.*

"Ready?" she asks me after she slides her feet into a pair of black flip-flops, but it's like a foghorn in my ears. She's also not wearing a bra, and her nipples are pebbled under the thin fabric.

Puppies... grandmas... Babe Ruth's baseball stats.

I need a cold shower.

"Archer?" She snaps me out of my thoughts.

"Oh." I clear my throat. "Yeah, ready to go?

"Yeah," she replies as she looks at me strangely. I decide the best way to go about that is to ignore it completely, so I pull open the door to the villa and hold it for her.

"After you."

"Thanks," she says. "What do you think you're going to get to eat?"

"I don't know," I answer. "I'll know it when I see it. What about you?"

"I'm thinking like every appetizer there is. I just want junk."

"And tequila," I add.

"Definitely tequila."

"Hell yes, let's do it." I'm all game for it. I usually don't allow myself to splurge on things like cheese fries and fajita nachos, but it's vacation, and Bay needs comfort food.

An hour later, we're sitting at a small, round-top table for two with every appetizer on the menu in front of us. We have oysters, crab legs, a cheese and fruit plate—you name it, it's here, along with two huge tequila sunrises.

After dinner, I can tell it wasn't enough. Bayleigh needs something more, and what that is, I don't know. All I know is tequila won't fix it, but it'll cause something else to hurt in the morning.

I sign the check and push my chair back. The look on her face says she thinks we'll go back to the room so she can stew in her own misery. *Well, no can do, missy.*

I hold my hand out for her, and she pushes her chair back and takes my hand. I lead her through the restaurant to the bar on the beach. It's like one of those tiki bars, and I see good things for my plans for the rest of the evening.

"What?" she asks, but I don't answer her. Instead, I pull two barstools toward one end of the bar. She climbs up, and I signal for the bartender.

"What can I do for you tonight?" she asks us before her eyes widen a bit when she sees Bayleigh, who flinches.

"I think we need two shot glasses and a bottle of tequila," I reply.

"I think so too," she says before moving to gather what we asked for.

"Archer?" Bayleigh asks quietly, and I hate the sad tone of her voice.

"It's all going to be okay, Bay," I tell her. "Promise."

"Okay," she says, and my heart stings a little bit. I love that she trusts me so much. I would do anything for her. Even get stupid-drunk on piss-poor tequila to make her feel better.

"Here you go," the bartender says as she sets down a bottle of bright-gold tequila, two shot glasses, a salt shaker, and a little bowl of lime wedges. My stomach burns already.

"Thanks," I tell her before turning to Bayleigh. "Ready?"

"Yeah."

We both lick our wrists, and I sprinkle salt on them. I fill our glasses with the powerful potion and push hers closer to her.

"Here goes nothing."

We pick up our glasses and lick the salt, shoot the tequila, and then bite the limes. I cringe, because this is not my favorite and never has been, but it also gets the job done. Bayleigh gasps. She's never been a good drinker.

I fill our glasses up.

"Again."

"Lick, shoot, suck!" she shouts before we throw back more tequila, and the room spins a bit.

Everyone around our end of the bar cheers. We've gained a lot of new friends. The kind who like people who get drunk and do stupid shit while on vacation. I can't remember, but I'm fairly sure they're why I no longer have clothes on and instead a grass skirt.

The song on the jukebox changes, and it's one I love, so I begin dancing right where I am, but that's not good enough. I jump up on the bar and give the good patrons and waitstaff a show of all my bits and pieces. But who cares, right?

"All right, cowboy." Bayleigh laughs. "I think we're probably done for the night."

"Fine, fine." I chuckle as I jump down from the bar.

We make our way back to the bungalow, both sufficiently drunk.

Once we're back in the room, away from prying eyes, Bayleigh pushes me up against the wall and whispers, "Kiss me." And I do. I kiss her like I've wanted to since this not-honeymoon started.

I turn us around so *her* back is to the wall and lift her up so we're eye level. I need to see her eyes to make sure she's on board with this. When she nods, silently answering my question, I press my mouth to hers and kiss her again. This time everywhere. Her neck. The top of her breast. I pull down the straps of her dress just slightly so I can kiss her shoulder. When I do, she lets out a moan. "Don't stop," she whispers into my ear and begins kissing my neck.

Why did we wait so long to do this?

FOURTEEN

Bayleigh

"**D**on't stop," I plead. I don't know what the change is in Archer, but I don't want him to stop. I need this. I need *him*.

I feel his hard length pressed against my center as he trails his mouth down the side of my neck and over the swells of my breasts. I wrap my legs tight around his waist and arch into him. I need… *more*.

He grabs my dress at my hips and shimmies it out from between my body and the wall. Archer raises it over my head and tosses it to the floor before leaning forward and putting his mouth over my nipple, sucking it deep into his mouth, making me arch into him, pushing and pulling at the connection. The movement abrades my pussy with his still-covered cock.

Archer kisses and licks his way back up my neck and covers my mouth with his, grinding his hips into mine. I slide my hands up his chest, his shirt somewhere long gone with his pants, and all he's wearing is a grass skirt. I'm thankful for his lack of clothing now. I rake my nails down his boxed abs, and he groans into my mouth, which only drives me higher. I feel him where I need him the most. But I need more. I don't want anything between us anymore. Never again.

I need to feel him touch me everywhere, and I need to do the same.

I feel a little clumsy as I fumble with the tie on his grass skirt, but I don't care. The only thing I care about right now is Archer and being with him, chasing this climax together.

Eventually, I pull the string just right, and the mix of palm fronds and other greenery falls limp. The only thing keeping it up is where it's balanced over the spot where our bodies are pressed together. I pull on it until it tugs free and toss it to the floor. I need to touch him, to feel the heat and the hardness of him in my hands, and then I need him inside me. But before I can get my hands on him, Archer gently grabs my wrist.

"Not yet," he says as he stops my hand. "It'll be over too fast if you touch me now."

I don't say anything; I just nod, because I'm with

him every step of the way. I need him too much to go back now.

He holds me tight to him, keeping my body wrapped around his as he carries me to the bed and slowly lowers me to my feet, the hard parts of his body scraping against the soft ones of mine. He presses his lips to mine and licks inside. I hold onto his shoulders and lean into our kiss, into him.

The way Archer looks at me has me flushing hot all over and feeling more than a little exposed, but before I can put too much thought into it, he scoops me up into his arms like the bride I wasn't and carries me the rest of the distance to the bed, where he lays me down in the center of it.

He looks me over and sees every inch of me, *and I want him too*. I watch him as he stands naked before me. Every inch of him is more delicious real estate of tan, toned skin. His cock is long and thick and hard. It juts out from his body, and he wraps his hand around the very base of him and strokes himself while he watches me.

"Ace," I whisper. I need him. *I need him now*, and he seems to understand the words I'm unable to voice.

"That's right, Bay; it's me," he says as he climbs up onto the bed between my legs. "Only me."

"Yes," I whisper.

Archer grabs the lace of my panties and slowly drags them down my legs. He pushes my thighs wider and stares at the very heart of me.

"Are you ready for me, Bayleigh?" he asks, his voice low and rough with sex.

"Yes."

"Mmm," he hums as he traces my sex with a fingertip. "Such a pretty pussy, all pink and wet for me."

"Please, Archer," I beg.

"What is it you need?" Archer asks me as he thrusts the digit into my center, making my gasp.

I swallow down my nervousness and answer him boldly, "I need you to fuck me."

"Gladly."

He covers my body with his, bracing his weight on his hands so he doesn't crush me. I feel him line up his cock with my opening and painstakingly push all the way inside me.

He rocks his hips into mine, and I hold onto him, digging my nails into his shoulders as he increases his pace. He presses his mouth to mine as he drives in and out, our bodies joining together, lighting my body up from the inside out.

Archer stops right before both of us hit our climax, and I moan out of frustration. "Stay with me. We're not done yet; I just want this to last longer, and I've wanted you too much for it to be over so fast."

I don't have the capacity to deal with that comment at the moment. My sole focus is on Archer and what we're doing. I just nod and follow his lead.

He slithers back down my body, shouldering my thighs apart as he settles in, worshiping my pussy like it's the last thing he's ever going to eat. I feel his tongue spear me, and I gasp. I don't know whether to pull him to me or try to crawl away. It's too much, and yet, I still want more and more and more. So I decide to quit fighting it and pull him to me.

When I twist my fingers in his hair, he moans, and *oh. My. Fucking. God.*

That was the straw. I come, and it's the most glorious thing I think I've ever experienced.

Once I catch my breath just a little, I realize Archer is now crawling back up my body, waiting for me to focus on him. "Better now?"

"Yeah," I whisper. My legs are still shaking, so he waits for me to steady myself, then begins kissing me all over again.

I feel him once more at my center, and I wrap myself around him and hold on tight as he drives in deep.

He plunges in and out. In and out. Driving as deep as he can go, joining our bodies and then pulling almost all the way out to the very tip of him. Only to slam back into me over and over. He fucks me like it's our last night on earth. It's rough and it's dirty. It's delicious, and I love every fucking second of it.

"I need you to get there," he growls.

"I'm there, baby," I tell him as I hold on tight. "I'm there."

"Then fucking come," he growls, and I do. This time, it doesn't need to build, because I was already there, and it washes over me. Archer plunges into me again and again, riding through my climax before driving in deep and staying there as he comes.

We hold each other, our mouths just barely touching as we breathe each other in.

When he slides out of me, separating us, it suddenly feels like a piece of me is missing.

He gives me one last kiss, before saying, "I need to go get cleaned up. You okay?"

I nod and watch him walk away, and then I promptly fall asleep in a drunk haze, hoping I remember this when I wake up in the morning. By far the best night of my life.

FIFTEEN

SWORN OFF

Archer

Fuuuck. My head is pounding. What happened last night?

The last thing I remember is… tequila. Lots of tequila… and dancing on a bar? In a grass skirt. Then... kissing Bayleigh. *Shit*. I kissed Bayleigh.

I look down and see I'm naked, but the bed is empty. I hear Bay in the bathroom, rustling around. "Shit," she whisper-shouts like she's mad but trying not to wake me up. She doesn't know I'm already awake. I hold perfectly still and continue to lie in bed so I can see if she says anything else. What the hell happened last night anyway?

When about ten minutes roll by, I decide to get out of bed. I take the sheet with me to cover myself up and try to find my boxers.

Looking around the room, I remember that I left them somewhere along the way at the tiki bar during our night of drinking and fucking, all that I have left as a memento is the grass skirt I wore last night, as it lays in a crumpled heap with Bayleigh's dress.

Bayleigh's dress. *Fuck me running, that dress.*

I remember pulling it off her. Kissing down her body. Beautiful and much better than any image I've ever dreamed of. The memory of carrying her over to the bed and worshiping her body like the queen she is. Like everything I ever wanted to do to her, but dismissed every time, because we've always just been *friends*. Friends who never, ever crossed that line. That is, we didn't until last night.

I have to piss like a racehorse, so I walk into the bathroom and see Bayleigh getting ready and packing at the same time. I don't know what to say or do. I feel awkward and uncomfortable like a thirteen-year-old getting caught with a stiffy in the community pool on a crowded summer day. This is new territory. We crossed a line we can never go back from. Good or bad, this will change our friendship forever.

"Hey," she breaks the silence.

"Morning." I look over to the opposite side of the room, worried if I make eye contact I'll see something

I don't want to see in her eyes—regret. That's the last thing I want, and it would gut me if I did.

"Ace," she says the nickname she's had for me since we were kids, and it almost sounds like a question. I finally nut up and look at her. The expression on her face is not one of regret. There's apprehension there. I'm sure the look on my face is the exact same. "We need to be at the shuttle for the airport in an hour."

I nod. It won't take me long to pack. Everything that's still clean, I'll roll up and stick on one side of my suitcase, and everything that's dirty, I'll wad up on the other side. I'm like a well-oiled machine.

"Okay. I'm going to jump in the shower real fast." I take a deep breath and start walking toward the stall.

But before I enter, she asks, "You okay?"

"Yeah, I'm good," I toss over my shoulder. I'm going to continue to avoid talking about the big, fat elephant in the room. "You?"

"Just nervous about going home to the mess," she answers, and I guess we're going to treat last night like Fight Club. And *everyone* knows the first rule of Fight Club. "I'm sure things will be fine."

"I sure hope so. The producers will be pissed if my drama eclipses the premiere of the movie." She sighs.

"Maybe it will be one of those *all press is good press* things and actually boosts visibility."

She shrugs. "Maybe."

I can tell she's nervous about returning to Sunnyville, but I don't know how to comfort her. I don't know how to make things right. For the first time in my life, I can't help but wonder if maybe they won't be.

We finish getting ready in awkward silence. Dancing around each other like we shared a one-night stand and didn't know each other until last night.

A few hours later, we're back at Fa'a'ā International Airport waiting for our flight back to the States. My stomach is growling, and I don't really want plane food. "We should grab dinner. The food on the plane kinda sucks."

"Yeah, that sounds good. What are you wanting?" she asks.

"There's not a lot of options," I realize as I'm looking at the map kiosk. "Let's go with that one." I point to the French Polynesian restaurant. "Nothing will top the food we had at the resort, but this will still probably be better than what we'll get on the flight."

"True." She nods. "Plus, it's our last chance for one more good meal before we get home. Let's do it."

Once we have our food, we find an empty table and take our seats.

"I'm so ready to be home." I'm truly missing my bed and my dogs.

"Me too." She looks over at the people rushing to get to their flights. "I'm glad we got here in plenty of time. I hate running late for a flight."

I nod. "Same. One time I was running late to a flight

out of DFW to San Francisco, and it was a hot mess. My luggage didn't make it onto the plane, so I landed with nothing but what I had on me. It took them three days to get it to me, and by then I was flying back home."

"Gross." She scoffs. "That sounds awful."

"It was," I agree.

Before either of us can say more, the lady comes on the loudspeaker and says in multiple languages that our flight is ready to board. "That's us," Bay says matter-of-factly.

"Yup." I nod and begin gathering the trash on our table to throw away before heading to our flight.

Once we make it to our seats, Bayleigh throws her headphones on, effectively letting me know she's not down for anymore awkward small talk. I should be mad, but I'm not. We both still need to process what happened last night.

We're finally back in Texas and driving home after the long-ass flight. The layover in San Francisco was brutal. We landed bright and early after the overnight flight where neither of us slept and had three hours until our flight to Dallas. I've never felt more tired than I do now. Not even after pulling all-nighters in vet school.

"I'm so ready to be home," I say.

"Oh my gosh. Me too." Bayleigh sighs. "I'm taking a nap as soon as I get to my parents' house."

"Me too, but at my house with my wieners."

Bayleigh laughs. I love that I make her smile. It's also no lie. I miss my bitches.

"What? They're the best snuggle dogs in the world." I'm pretending to be offended, but really the wiener jokes never get old.

"I bet they miss you," she says sadly. I know she hasn't had the time in her schedule back in Los Angeles to have a pet. Bay hasn't had one in years, and that makes me sad to think about, because when she was a girl, she could never have enough and loved them all.

"Nah, they get super spoiled by Evan. She gives them way too many treats. I keep trying to limit how much Daphne eats. She's crazy overweight, but that's what happens when you have a lazy Doxie." I shrug. Seriously though. She's had like thirty-five puppies. As a vet, I know she's too fat, but then as her human, I know she deserves to eat and nap all day. *The struggle is real.*

I rescued Lily and Daphne from a puppy mill that had gotten shut down for animal cruelty. I understand wanting a purebred dog. Sometimes, they're needed, but there are so many animals out there that need good homes. And most of them are the sweetest animals and just need some love. I wish more people knew the truth of puppy mills and how to research reputable breeders.

It's a pet project of mine to help take the dogs rescued from puppy mills and let them go to trainers at an organization called Purple Paws. They make sure the dogs that pass through their doors have all the training they need to go on to a good life as a PTSD service dog for veterans. My buddies from vet school and I like to call it Vets Helping Vets.

We continue chatting about the wieners and the funny things they do. And Bay's movie and the auditions for her next potential projects. The urge to grab Bayleigh's hand is there. If I learned anything from our night together, it's that she's perfect for me. The sex was explosive in all the right ways. We were drunk, so I can only imagine how it would be when we're not. But I know that can never happen again. I just hope the one slip doesn't ruin what we have when we finally get back to our non-honeymoon lives. Bayleigh will go back to L.A. soon, and I'm worried I will never see her again. We've always kept in touch and meet up when she's in town, but that was before we slept together. Now, there's no telling what she'll do. Maybe she'll ignore it and pretend it never happened, or maybe she'll cut and run.

When we finally pull into Bayleigh's parents' driveway, it seems like the weight of the world is back on her shoulders. She still hasn't turned on her phone to check on anything. I doubt she wants to. The article from douchebag Paul is supposed to be released tomorrow, and only time will tell what will happen from there.

I get out of the car at the same time Bay does. I pull her bags out of the trunk and carry them up to the porch for her.

"Thank you," she says, her voice filled with meaning. "Thank you so much for coming with me."

"Anything for you, Bay." And I mean it. I would do anything for her, now even more so.

I'm thankful my dad let me jet off for ten days. He was able to pull in one of the retired vets in town to fill in for things while I was gone to cover my ass and my patients of the paw and hoof variety.

"I know." She smiles, but it doesn't reach her eyes. The carefree Bayleigh I've known all my life is gone, and this Bayleigh I've never seen before is in her place.

About the time we reach the front door, Bayleigh's mom, Liv, comes outside. "Oh my goodness! Y'all are finally back. How was it?"

"Hey, Mom. Oh my gosh, it was amazing," Bayleigh says as she reaches her and gives her a big hug.

"I'm so glad!" She turns to pull me into a hug next. "Hey, Archer."

"Hey, Mrs. Hart," I say politely.

"Mrs. Hart?" she questions. "Archer, how long have you known me? Why do you still call me Mrs. Hart?"

"It's a habit." I laugh. "Drilled into me since I was a kid. And if I quit now, my momma would still beat me."

She laughs with me. "I know she would, dear. Oh I

know."

About that time, I hear barking coming from inside and realize Lily and Daphne are here.

"Oh, Evan brought them over here this morning. She didn't want them to be left alone all day when she was working." She walks over to the door and opens it, and they come running out. They're both crying when they see me.

"Hello, my precious angels!" I say, picking up Lily so she can climb up my chest and lick my face as much as she wants. This is the longest I've been away from them since getting them. Daphne is loving on Bayleigh. They bonded when she figured out the way to Daph's heart is getting pets first and rubbing her belly. Otherwise, she'll cut you.

"Yes, yes. I love you too, Lily," I say to her before putting her down to show some love to my other girl.

Once they've calmed down, I look over at Bayleigh, and you can tell she's exhausted. It's in every inch of her and the cute little creases between her brows on her forehead. I am too.

"Well, I'm going to get back home. Thanks for taking me with you, Bay."

She smiles and comes in for a hug. "No, thank you for going with me. I needed that, and I'm glad you were there and not Paul."

I nod and hug her back awkwardly. I grab the wieners and put them in my car to get to my house. It's not far, right next door to be exact, but these lazy little hussies don't even like to walk that far.

I bought this house shortly after my dad brought me on full-time after my residency in central Texas. I will eventually take over the vet clinic when he retires, but I'm really enjoying working with him. We've always been close, and now it's something we both share.

I pull the girls out of the car and set them down on the ground. They follow me around to the back of the car to get my luggage, then into the house, which Evan must've cleaned for me, because it's spotless. I need to thank her later with an amazing gift, but dinner and bed are priorities. I don't have any food in the fridge, so I decide to call in an order to one of the local restaurants for pickup. No one delivers this far out in the country. It's one of the very few downers to country living.

Once I'm done eating, I shower and go to bed. This is the first time I've had a chance to really reflect on what happened between me and Bayleigh, but I'm so exhausted I'm asleep within minutes.

I spend the night dreaming of Bayleigh and her beautiful body. And the damn truth is that it's probably the only place I will get to see it ever again. I've got to fix our friendship and move on from that night, and the only way to do it is to pretend like it never happened… *starting tomorrow*.

SIXTEEN

JUST THE TIP

Bayleigh

What am I going to do?

I would be lying if I said I haven't found myself in a few jams throughout my life, but I've never been in this big of a pickle before. A little less than two weeks ago, I was engaged to one man, and now I'm not, wondering when I fell in love with my best friend, because I have no idea.

He was just so weird. Archer barely looked me in the eyes when he dropped me off and drove away as fast as he could. It would have been a little more climactic if he didn't live next door.

Oh my God, this is all so awkward.

Somehow, I managed to sleep with my best friend, the man that I've had feelings for longer than I can remember, and by his cut-and-run performance, I can only assume he doesn't feel the same way. Sure, I knew I had a crush on him when we were younger, but now there's no doubt about how I feel. Waking up next to a naked Archer was like getting struck by lightning. I'm forever changed with a brand on my heart and the ability to predict the weather. Okay, the first is true; the second is an exaggeration.

To make matters worse, I knew. I knew he was a hound, and I slept with him anyway. I guess after years and years of watching him blow through women like a box of tissues I figured that if we ever came together, it would be magical like a fairy tale and not a train wreck. I never thought he'd hit it and quit… *me*.

Last night, I thought that after catching up on some sleep and a decent breakfast I'd have a better handle on the situation. But as I sit on the porch in a pair of old sweats with my feet up on the painted-white railing around my childhood home, I know I'm no closer to answers than I was last night.

I raise my coffee mug to my lips and look over at Archer's house. It's dark and empty. He left for work early this morning, long before I stopped tossing and turning and decided to take the bull by the horns. Or in this case, the man by the ear and remind him he's not running from me. We're talking this out, and if it leads to more spectacular orgasms, then that's the play we're running. But when I walked downstairs ready to seize the day, it was clear he seized it first.

Archer is avoiding me, and if this is an attempt to scrape me off, I don't like it one bit.

I hear a car approaching and look up in time to see Evan's classic Mustang pull into the driveway of Archer's house. His little sister is a wild one and always has been, but in the very best of ways. She's been one of my oldest friends along with her brother. And now I can't help but wonder, if I screwed up with one, would I lose the other too?

The thought causes my heart to pang, but I snicker to myself as I hear her open the front door and then bite out a "shit" as Daphne makes a break for it. She runs down the driveway and up the walk to my parents' front door, where she frantically scratches the wood panel until my mom opens the door.

"Well hello, sweet girl," she says. "Come for a visit, have you?"

She ushers the little sausage doggie into the house and shuts the door before Evan opens the front door again just in time for Lily to race out and down the steps, up the walk, and over to me, where I scoop her up and pull her into my lap. She settles in and makes herself comfy as Evan spies her and rolls her eyes. I'm fairly sure she says the word "hussy" under her breath, but she's too far away for me to hear, and I haven't had enough coffee to try to read lips yet.

I raise my mug up to my mouth and take a big swig of coffee right as she marches up the steps of my parents' front porch.

"So," she starts as soon as I've taken another big sip of coffee, "I take it you've seen my brother's wiener."

My eyes go wide as I try to swallow down the coffee, but I gasp at the realization that Evan knows Archer and I slept together. Shit, shit, shit. Is she mad? Does she hate me? Will she still be my friend? I wonder if she pities me because her brother doesn't feel the same way. Oh God. This is terrible.

"Jesus H. I didn't mean to make you choke," she says as she slaps me on the back really hard, making Lily growl her pitiful little yappy growl. "I just figured since you have Lily, you know where Daphne is."

Fuck me, she meant the dog. She has no idea about Archer and me, and I aim to keep it that way until I figure out how I'm going to find my way out of this current mess.

"She's in the house with Mom," I croak and cough out the last of the coffee that filled my windpipe.

"That's fucking gross," Evan says.

"And you're molding the minds of America's future with that foul mouth," I reply with a smile and roll my eyes. "Shame."

"Maybe you'd be nicer if you got laid more," she tells me before nodding to the pup in my lap. "You should touch more wieners than my brother's."

"Just the tip!" I laugh as I boop Lily on the nose with a fingertip.

"You're ridiculous." Evan laughs at me. "I love you, you know?"

"I know," I answer. I wasn't sure, but it's nice to hear. "I love you too."

"You're really okay?" she asks me. "You know, with Dr. Douchebag being Cheating Dr. Douchebag and all that?"

"Yeah," I say with a sigh. "I don't think I really loved him. I think he was all I thought I could get, but I deserve better."

"Hell yeah, you do!" she cheers. "I hope it's with someone who doesn't think you eat pussy like you chew a piece of bubble gum. I swear the last guy I dated bit me, and not in the fun kinda kinky way either."

"You're a little disgusting." I laugh.

"I know." She winks at me. "Isn't it great?"

"What do the parents think about you?"

"Eh," she answers. "They love me. I get it all out of my system after hours so I don't make any slips at work. Besides, I have to mind my Ps and Qs. Rumor has it, they finally hired a new superintendent after the last one ran off to Boca with his secretary."

"For a second, I think I forgot how wild Sunnyville really is."

"Yeah, it's a real thrill a minute."

There's something about the look on her face that bothers me. I've been so wrapped up in myself and Archer that I didn't really pay much attention to Evan until now.

"Are you okay?" I ask her.

"Of course," she lies. "Why wouldn't I be?"

"You never acted like you hated Sunnyville before," I say hesitantly.

"Oh, I don't," she replies immediately, and she looks almost back to her regular self. "Not really. I just… I don't know."

"What is it, doll?"

"I just have been kind of lonely, and I didn't realize it until you came home and you and Archer have been connected at the hip the whole time," she explains. "It feels kind of like I don't have anyone."

"You have me."

"Oh don't be silly," she says. "I'm fine."

"I mean it, Evan," I tell her. "You have me too."

"I know," she replies, and she forces herself to brighten. "I should go collect my brother's wayward wiener from your mother."

"You couldn't help yourself, could you?" I ask.

"Absolutely not."

"Good." I laugh. "Don't ever change."

"I wasn't planning on it." She winks before she scoops Lily up out of my lap and disappears into the house to collect Daphne from my mom, who is probably two seconds away from hoisting the chunky dachshund into a stroller and pushing her through the neighborhood for a morning walk like a baby doll. The thought makes me laugh, although I really wouldn't put it past my mother.

Evan takes the dogs back to Archer's house, leaving me all alone with nothing to do but plot against a wayward veterinarian who owes me an explanation.

SEVENTEEN

THE FARMER AND THE BELLE

Archer

I t's been a long day of dealing with farm animals. Had to rush out to one of the local farms to help deliver a calf that was stuck. It was touch and go there for a bit; I thought we lost momma, but she pulled through. She was tired, but she's being a mom now and feeding her sweet baby.

Dad sent me home after that. It was almost closing time anyway, but I was covered in blood and dirt, and the last few fur parents didn't need to see that.

I'm thankful for the long day. It's kept my mind off Bayleigh and the possibility of her completely leaving and never coming back because of me and my drunken stupidity. I should've stopped it. I should've never even kissed her when she asked me to, but I did. I didn't know that I wanted her, or how much I did, until I had her and I knew there was no going back. Sure, I was attracted to my best friend, she's hot, but just because she's hot doesn't mean I needed to get my dick wet when she wouldn't have meant anything and it would have ruined our friendship. But now? Now I know fucking better.

When I get home, I let the wieners outside to play in the backyard while I jump in the shower. They're happy to just sunbathe and live life.

In the shower, I'm left with my thoughts on how to try to fix this between Bayleigh and me. Do I confront it head-on? Pretend like it never happened? Try to do it again?

That last thought is the most appealing.

Instead, I go for ignoring it—for now.

I go about my evening routine, dinner, research on a difficult case we had today, and an episode of a show I've been trying to watch on Netflix.

When I'm sitting on my sofa in my empty house, I realize how lonely I am. It's never bothered me before. I enjoy being by myself usually, but all of a sudden, the silence and no one to talk to is deafening.

I'm sure being with someone twenty-four seven for the last ten days has a lot to do with that. We had a lot of fun. Many times, just being next to each other while she read and I either watched television or went for a swim.

Having her there just seemed natural. It worked. And it's something I could get used to.

Only, that's not possible.

One: She's totally shut me out.

Two: She's an actress who will go far and will live a big-time life.

Three: She won't have time for a small-town veterinarian.

Not that there's anything wrong with the last two. I'm proud of her. I'm proud of how far she's gone. It was her lifelong dream to act. And she's done it. This movie role is going to be her big break. It wouldn't surprise me if the offers for new roles are rolling in on the hour. And she deserves everything she's ever wanted. Even if it means she's going to be out of my life for good and not just in the periphery. Maybe it'll be better this way. Maybe now I'll be able to find my own way with the door to Bayleigh firmly closed.

I'm pulled out of my own head when my phone vibrates. It's my sister.

> **Evan: Does Bayleigh seem off to you today?**

> **Me: I haven't seen her today. She's probably just tired. Plus, that dumb article was supposed to come out today.**

> **Evan: Oh, she didn't even mention that.**

> **Me: She may not have even looked at it.**

I haven't looked myself. And she kept her phone off basically our entire trip. Her agent had to call her at our hotel.

Evan: Probably not then. I haven't looked. Maybe we should.

At that, I toggle over to my browser app on my phone, and that's when I see the headline: PLASTIC SURGEON TO THE STARS OPENS UP ABOUT HIS RUNAWAY BRIDE, BAYLEIGH HART.

What little I know about tabloids and whatnot makes me laugh. The fact that they did not use his name at all and highlighted hers is fucking hilarious. They're using her to boost ratings, not him. He was clearly using her name to make one for himself. Bay was always a brighter star than she realized.

I skim through the story, and it's literally him whining about her dumping him at their wedding to run off with some "dumb farmer" to their honeymoon he paid for. Only he didn't pay for shit. Bayleigh's parents paid for the wedding, and Bayleigh paid for the honeymoon herself.

My phone buzzes with another text.

Evan: Dude. That was literally nothing. (laugh emoji)

Me: I just read it too. And laughed. Called me a dumb farmer.

Evan: Weeelll, Dad did say you pulled a

calf from her momma today.

Me: That I did, sis.

Evan: Pretty farmer-y to me. Mooo. (laugh emoji) (cow emoji)

Me: Shut up.

I laugh and put my phone down and wonder if Bayleigh has seen it. Cause she'll get a kick out of it too. And I'm sure it's boosting ratings for the film as well. I decide to take my chances and shoot her a text.

Me: Did you see the article? It's a lot of nothing; I promise.

I wait a good ten minutes of not getting a reply back before I decide to walk over to the Hart house to see her myself.

When I get to the front door, all seems quiet. Looks like no one is home, but I knock anyway. A few seconds go by, and I don't hear a peep, so I head back home.

They're probably out for dinner, so I do my best not to worry. At least I know she's being taken care of. Mr. and Mrs. Hart are some of the most amazing people I know. They'd do anything for their daughter. And I would too. In a heartbeat.

I don't know when I truly started feeling this way. Some part of me thinks I always have, but I needed to look past the friendship part of us and see her not as the little girl anymore, but as a woman. A heartbreakingly beautiful woman.

I opt to text Bayleigh one more time to let her know I'm here when she's ready to talk before I grab my wieners and head off to bed.

The next day, I'm back at work. Today is our house-pets-only day. We usually don't see farm animals on these days unless there's an emergency, so I brought Lily and Daphne with me. They love it up here. Daphne stays under the desk with my mom, and Lily walks around like she's the big dog on campus. All six pounds of her. She loves hanging out with the dogs that come in for their checkups. It helps them get used to other dogs as well.

We finally have a break in the schedule before lunch, and my dad and I are cleaning up the stations in the back. "You good, son?"

"Yeah, why?" I ask.

"You've just been real quiet today. It's not like you." He's right though. I've been off all day. Obviously, I've been acting happy with the patients' parents, but in between, I'm back to zombie mode.

"Just tired from vacation," I lie. And he knows I'm lying. Well, kinda. I am still jetlagged, but that's not why I'm acting off today.

"Did something happen between you and Bayleigh?" he questions. Of course he's right on the mark, but I'm not prepared to tell him that yet. I avoid looking at him for fear he'll see it on my face. "It did, didn't it?"

I brave a look at him, expecting him to be disappointed in me, but instead, I'm greeted with a smirk. I nod. "Yeah, something happened."

"'Bout damn time."

Wait, what?

"Huh?"

"Son, you two have loved each other since you were kids," he states matter-of-factly. He's not wrong, but I still did not see that coming.

"Yeah, but as friends." I can feel the lie in my words as they leave my mouth. I grab the back of my neck, trying to hide my nervousness. 'Cause I know he's right.

"Love that starts with friendship can turn out to be one of the strongest bonds. That girl is head-over-heels in love with you. I was shocked when we got her wedding invitation in the mail a month ago." He pats me on the back. "Have you talked to her since you've been back?" I shake my head. "Well, give her a few more hours or so to think things through and deal with the fallout from her wedding, then go after her."

I look at him again, stunned he's saying this. I always thought I'd kept my feelings for Bay locked down. Apparently, not as well as I thought I had.

Before I can say anything, he starts again. "I mean it, son. Don't let her get away a second time. You won't be so lucky the next time around."

The rest of the day is the same mundane things, which allows me to just run on autopilot and not think about the revelations my dad spilled or the fact that Bayleigh hasn't called or texted or anything, and that's something we used to do daily. Just a simple *"Hey, what's up?"* check-in.

She's staying literally next door to me, and this is now the longest we've gone without talking. Even when she's in California, we would call and text or even send a goddamn e-mail when needed.

I don't like it.

In fact, I absolutely *hate* it. I hate this new awkwardness between us. I hate that she feels she has to leave her phone off. I make a pact with myself that I am going to fix this. Us. *Tonight.*

EIGHTEEN

MONKEY WRENCH

Well, shit. That is not what I planned.

I had thought that I was going to hunt Archer down and make him come to terms with what happened between us—and what was going to continue to happen, if I had anything to say about it. I was ready to take this bull by the horns, but then my phone rang. And it rang and it rang and it rang.

I had forgotten all about Paul's tell-all that was supposed to be in one of the tabloids, and it was. It was actually a little anticlimactic. Apparently, they did a photoshoot, and he looked exactly how he turned out to be in real life—a douchebag. In the interview, all he did was whine about how I didn't do enough to elevate his business with my industry contacts and the name that I had built for myself. And that's not even the best part.

About halfway through the article, when the interviewer asked him about our bust of a wedding, he told the world that I left him at the altar in the middle of the ceremony and ran away with Archer—well, he called him a small-town hick farmer, but that's semantics. Everything but that jab was true.

When they asked him why I ran away from our wedding, he had the perfect opportunity to paint me as the bad guy and come off looking like a hero, but Paul is dumber than I originally thought. Instead, he told the world that it was because I had found out about his mistress—which, sadly, is still true. My favorite part though was that I had driven him into the arms of another by being a crappy girlfriend.

With my phone ringing off the hook, I was positive this was nothing but bad news, and I wasn't even sure I was going to weather this particular storm. I was beginning to think I needed the Help Wanted section out of the local paper. Maybe someone needed a receptionist or a babysitter.

Clearly, my work in Hollywood was over.

Going through my text messages, I realize my agent has texted me to call her fifteen thousand times, so I check that off my list first. She wants to meet with me when I'm in Hollywood next week for the premiere.

Something about a ton of good offers coming in.

The rest of the text messages are people telling me how brave I am to dump the douchebag at the altar.

I smile and laugh inwardly. Serves him right.

Apparently, I was wrong. My career isn't over; it's just beginning.

I'm both excited and nervous at the same time.

I had my agent send in an audition tape of me when I was in Bora Bora to a few different directors looking for women who look like me. And a few who didn't have particular descriptions but just wanted a good actress.

I would love to land another huge blockbuster, but now that my feelings for Archer are out in the universe, I don't know. Could I have the chance at more? With the one man I've always loved? Do I really want to be traveling like that while trying to start a family—assuming Archer even wants that?

Maybe I was just a one-night thing for him? Maybe that will never happen again.

"You okay, Bay?" I jump at the sound of my mom's voice.

"Crap, you scared the beejubus out of me."

"I'm sorry." She giggles. "I just wanted to make sure you were okay.

"Yup, I'm good."

"Good. Do you mind if your dad and I come in here and watch one of our shows?" she asks sweetly.

"Mom, it's your house," I say. "You do what you

want."

"I know, dear, but I know you've been kinda struggling with some stuff since the wedding, and we want to give you as much space as you need."

I love my mom so much. Always so calm and considerate of others. I smile. "I don't need space. I'm good. You and Dad come watch your show."

"You sure?" she questions.

"One hundred percent. Mind if I watch it with you?"

My dad comes around the corner with a bowl of popcorn and a soda. "Not at all, Bay. Why don't you go grab you something to drink, and I'll get it pulled up on the TV."

I comply, and a few minutes later, I'm back with a huge glass of water and my own bowl of popcorn— 'cause I'm not the sharing type. I like my own.

I grab the blanket off the edge of the sofa and prepare to watch whatever my parents are watching.

It's one of those hospital dramas I can't stand, but I enjoy listening to my mom and dad talk back and forth about what ailment they think these people might have. The things these show writers come up with make me roll my eyes.

About thirty minutes into the show, there's a knock on the door. "I got it." I get up so my parents can continue watching. They're so engrossed they don't even pause it to see who it is.

I walk around the corner, and it's Archer. He smiles

when he sees it's me coming to the door, and my heart takes flight.

When I open the door, he doesn't even say hey before pushing me back against the wall and kissing me like his life depends on it.

NINETEEN

NICE & SLOW

Archer

grab her a little rougher than I intended, push her back up against the wall, and kiss her like my next breath depends on it.

"Archer," she whispers, and my name on her lips in this moment is fucking hot. I go in for more, but she stops me. "What are you doing?"

That's a good question. What am I doing? Now that I've had a taste of her, she's literally all I want. If she decides we can't do this, I will be a gentleman and walk away, but I will never be the same. *We* will never be the same.

When I don't answer, she says, "We just can't do it

here. My parents are in the living room."

"Oh," I reply as I push out a breath. I had completely forgotten about her parents. I just knew when she opened the door I had to touch her, taste her. I had forgotten about everything else and just let the rest of the world slip away. But that's also not smart. I can't get caught with my pants down in the middle of town, and neither can Bayleigh.

I grab her hand at the same moment she steps forward, and we make our way down the walkway and over to my house next door. I can't get the door unlocked fast enough.

When we're finally inside, we both just stare at each other. I can't believe she's here, in my house with me like this.

"Bay—" I start. I need to know if this is really happening, if she's here with me now, but before I can, she puts her finger to my lips, effectively cutting off the question.

"I don't want to talk anymore," she says, and it's all I need to know. I press my mouth to hers, and she opens underneath me, so I pour everything I can't say to her into my kiss.

She takes a step back to get to the wall, and I get us to where she wants to be. It takes me back to a few nights ago when we were in a similar position with nothing but the sounds of the ocean hitting our bungalow. This time though, Lily and Daphne are barking in the background, wanting to be let out of their room.

The barking is a solid mood killer, so I decide to let go and get them outside. At least they'll be fine hanging out there while I finally get my hands on Bayleigh again since our last night in Bora Bora.

I back away slightly and wait for her to look at me. "I should let the dogs out. Go make yourself at home, and I'll be right back."

Bayleigh nods, and I set myself off toward the dogs to get them outside. Their room is like a sunroom in the back of the house, so I'm able to let them out without them trying to love on Bayleigh before *I* get a chance to love on Bayleigh.

When I make it to the sunroom, the dogs go crazy. "Let's go outside, girls." They listen like the sweet, obedient dogs they are, and once they're outside and the door is firmly shut, I make my way back into the main part of the house to find Bay.

She's sitting on my leather sectional sofa, her legs tucked under her, and she just fits so perfectly in my home.

I make my way over to the sofa and take a seat next to her. She shuffles slightly so she's looking at me. I tuck a stray strand of hair behind her ear and leave my hand on her neck for a few seconds to see if the mood is gone before I lean in to kiss her again.

She backs off again after a few minutes, but only to swing her leg over me and settle on top. That puts me at the perfect position to place my hands on her hips to get her exactly where I want her when I feel her heat press against the front of my jeans.

She places her hands on my neck at the same time mine begin to explore her body.

I slowly slip my hands up, sliding her shirt up as I make my ascent. When I get to the elastic part of her bra, she brings her hands down and begins running them over my abs, lifting my shirt up in the process.

Bayleigh pulls back from our kiss, and for a moment, I'm worried she's going to ask to stop, but she doesn't.

She reaches for the hem of her shirt and pulls it over her head.

When I realize what she's doing, I grab the back of my collar and pull my T-shirt off. She starts to reach for her bra, but I stop her. This is mine, and I want it. I may only get this one more time, and I'm taking it.

"Ace," she whispers.

"Shhh… this is for me."

She understands and drops her hands, letting me reach behind her to unclasp the hooks in the back.

The material falls slack and does little now to cover her. I realize again just how beautiful she is. I've always known this, but not until our last night in Bora Bora did it really hit me that she's a different kind of beautiful. Bayleigh is a one of a kind woman and I was a fucking moron to not have seen how special she was until now.

But now I know and I'm not letting her go, am I?

I take a moment to drag my gaze over her body before kissing the top of her breast as I slip her bra the rest of the way down.

Bayleigh's head falls back, and she lets out a small moan.

I make my way down to her nipple while cupping the other breast in my left hand. When my lips hit her nipple, I open my mouth and bite down gently, and that gets a moan and a breathy "*Ace*" out of her. *Fuck yes.*

This moment is perfection. I'm getting to really explore her body the way that I've dreamed of—this time sober as a judge.

She pulls her head back again, and I reach up to the side of her face and pull her back in for a kiss. She rocks her hips against mine, riding up and down the length of me. If I wasn't already rock-hard, that would've done it.

In one swift motion, I place my hands under the back of her legs and stand up. She wraps her arms around me to hold on while I walk down the hall to my bedroom. I toe the door open the rest of the way and carry her to my bed like she's precious, like she's everything, and I gently set her in the middle of the big mattress.

She lets go at the same time I pull my arms out from underneath her, and she slides her hands up to the back of my neck as she pulls me toward her. My lips touch hers again, my hands moving over her body as she explores mine.

When her hands reach the top of my jeans, she pops the top button and promptly begins kissing her way down my chest. She stops way too soon, but it's only so she can stand up. When she does, I push my jeans down my legs and step out of them.

I push down my boxers and kick out of them. When my cock is free, I grip the base of it to slow things down a bit and look at Bayleigh. She licks her lips and walks back toward me, placing herself firmly between my legs. She picks up where we left off, her lips on my chest. She pays special attention to my abs, but when she gets down to my hipbone, she pauses for a second to look up at me and get on her knees.

This is the sexiest fucking thing I've ever seen.

Bayleigh on her knees with her mouth at my dick.

She gently places her hand slightly above mine and strokes it up and down. I let go and put my hands behind me on the bed.

I watch her as her tongue swipes the precum off the tip, and I'm a goner. My head falls back right at the same time she wraps her mouth around my cock and sucks. She bobs up and down. Up and down. I feel her hot mouth all around me.

This is too much. I don't want to blow right now. I want to explore her too.

"Bay." My breathing is heavy. "Stop." She does as I ask, and before she can think I wasn't into it, I show her I need more. I need to touch and taste her. And when I come, I want to be deep inside her, not a quick blow in her mouth.

She stands up, and I pull her in to kiss her while I work her yoga pants down her legs. My hands slide over her hips, successfully pushing them down to the ground where she kicks them off.

I lift her up and flip us around so she's on the bed and I'm standing in front of her, but that's not how I want her. "Scoot back and put your head on the pillows."

Without any fight, she does what I ask, and I follow her.

Bayleigh makes herself comfortable on the pillows, and I make my way onto the bed, pausing for a minute to look at her body—*beautiful*. She tries to cover herself, to hide from me, but I won't have it. I grab her hands and place them next to her. "Don't hide yourself from me. You're too perfect for that."

She doesn't say anything, but she no longer tries to hide from me either.

Before she can say anything, I lean down to kiss her again. I could seriously kiss her for eternity and be a happy man. But I want more. If this is my only chance to have her one last time, then I'm going to take it with no regrets.

I cover her body with mine, swirling my tongue around her nipple until it peaks, and I listen to the little noises she makes. I hear her breath catch in the back of her throat, and I know she likes the way I make her feel.

I lean my weight on one arm and use my free hand to trace lines up her leg slowly from her foot up to the spot I ultimately want to be. When I reach the apex of her thighs, she arches her back, instinctively trying to get closer to me.

The last time we did this, we were both drunk. We explored each other's body, but not near as thoroughly as we're doing right now. And I'm going to take my time this time.

I stop to look at her while I push two fingers inside her. She's so wet. So fucking wet for me.

"Ace," she moans. "Please don't stop."

And I don't. I pump my fingers in and out of her while I kiss and lick all the way down to her center. When I get to the top of her hipbone, she lifts off the bed slightly, trying to force me to where she wants me most. I smile and give my girl what she needs. *My girl*. I don't know when that happened, but I don't hate it. I guess in some way, she's always been mine.

When I reach her clit, I lick it slowly again and again, and I revel in every moan I can pull from her. These are my victories, and here, the winner takes all. I pump my fingers in and out while I consume her.

She threads her fingers through my hair and pulls. I love the sting and bite. It only encourages me to keep going while she chases her orgasm. But with me, she'll never have to chase anything. I'll give it to her freely over and over again.

I move my fingers and tongue faster and faster, pushing her until she reaches *that* point. When she comes, I don't stop. I gentle my movements so I can build it in her again. I'm not done with her yet.

"Mmmmmm…" she moans, the sweetest sound, when she comes down from her climax. "Come here."

I cover her with my body again, and she wraps her arms around my shoulders.

"What do you want?" I ask her, even though I already know.

"I need you inside me."

I smile. "Yes, ma'am."

She laughs. "Southern charm will always be a turn-on."

"I'll keep that in mind." I wink.

I guide myself to her entrance and slowly push in. She moans when we find our rhythm, and I lean down to take her mouth again.

I feel her walls flutter around me, and I'm so close, closer than I want to be to an orgasm before I can make her come again.

"Get there, baby," I pant as I drive into her over and over, our bodies crashing together.

"Yes," she pants, and I feel her tighten around me and my balls draw tight. I know that I won't be able to hold back. "Yes."

I know she's there; she's just as close as I am, and I pick up the pace, moving within her, driving deeper, harder, faster. I feel her nails break the skin of my back and I revel in it like a goddamn warrior. Her body bows backward and her mouth forms a beautiful little "o" as her pussy draws me in even deeper and holds me tight. I'm helpless to stop the pleasure coursing through me and with a shudder rolling through my body as I hold her tight, we come together.

I press my mouth to hers one last time before I pull out and roll from the bed. I make my way into the bathroom and grab a clean washcloth for Bay, running it under the warm faucet and wringing it out before carrying it back to my girl.

When I return to her, she's still in the same spot I left her in, her breathing still heavy, hair splayed across my pillow. "Beautiful."

"Hmmm…?" she questions, and I realize I said it out loud.

"I said you're beautiful."

She doesn't reply as I climb back on the bed and clean her up. I toss the washcloth back toward the bathroom and curl up with her in bed, turning her so we're both on our sides and I can pull her into me.

"What about the dogs?" Bayleigh asks, remembering we left them outside.

"They're fine. I left the door cracked so they could get back in. I'll go check on them in a second."

"Oh good," she says, voice raspy from sex.

"They'll be pissed if I leave them out there for the

night." I laugh. "They're snugglers."

We continue lying there in silence for a few more minutes before Bayleigh starts climbing out of bed. "I should get going."

And just like that, it's over. It's like a bucket of cold water has been dumped over me, and I remember Bayleigh is not mine to keep. I'm good to scratch an itch, but anything more than that would be inconvenient.

I try to hide the disappointment on my face. "Okay."

I want to tell her not to go, that she's mine and I'm keeping her. Instead, I throw on my boxers and a pair of workout shorts before I go get her shirt and bra out of the living room.

When I return, she's dressed minus the articles of clothing I'm holding.

She grabs them out of my hand and makes quick work putting her clothes back on, and things are awkward again. I fucking hate it.

"I'm ummm... heading back to L.A. tomorrow," she says as she pulls her shirt down over her body.

Fuck. I knew this was coming, but I didn't think it would be so soon. I guess I wasn't paying much attention when I was lost to the bliss of Bayleigh in my life and in my bed. "Oh, okay."

"The premiere is in a couple of days. Evan is going with me."

Fucking Evan. Of course my sister would go. Not that I could anyway after taking off ten days last minute to go to Bora Bora with Bay. "Cool. You guys will have fun." I grab the back of my neck.

"I'm sure we will," she says as I start walking her to the door to let her out. "Thank you, Ace," she adds as she comes in for a hug. This hug luckily isn't awkward.

"Anytime, Bay," I reply. And I mean it. If this is the only piece I'll ever get from her, I'll take it. Even though I want way more. But I'm not sure that's what she wants. Or what we can ever even have.

I walk her back to her parents in awkward silence to make sure she gets inside safely. She waves at me when she gets the door open, and I turn and go back to my house.

She's going back to L.A. Who knows when I'll get to see her again? This can't work between us. It's just not possible. Not with her half a country away. In a culture I will never understand.

TWENTY

STEP AND REPEAT

Bayleigh

I wake early the next morning to run through the coffee shop drive-thru before swinging over to Evan's cute little townhouse in the historic district of Sunnyville.

She's sitting outside on her front porch waiting when I pull up. I get out and immediately hand her the coffee before grabbing her bags to put in the trunk of my mom's SUV. "You are such a freaking lifesaver. Probably your own life, but…" She shrugs. "Whatever."

I laugh. "Same, girl, same. I live on coffee. I'd get an IV drip if I could."

She nods in agreement, then we both jump in the car and we're off.

We don't say a word to each other while we finish our coffee and the sun is up just a little more, but I finally break the silence. "What are you most looking forward to seeing when we're there?"

"Oh my gosh, I've been googling like a mad woman since my vacation was approved."

I laugh while she pulls out her phone with a list of things she wants to see, which surprises me, because she's usually a "fly by the seat of her pants" person.

"I know what you're thinking, Bay." I see her eyeing me out the corner of my eye. "This isn't an itinerary. It's just a list of things I want to see."

"Well, spill it," I tell her.

"I want to see Ellen's house, Adele's house, the Hollywood sign, the Hollywood Walk of Fame. I want to drive through Malibu, see the inside of a studio—I don't care which one…"

She continues to droll on excitedly. I don't think I've ever seen her this excited about anything. "Okay, okay." I laugh and stop her. "I get it; you want to see it all."

She nods. "Hell yeah, I do."

"We'll do what we can, but there's one thing missing off that list of yours," I say.

"What?"

"Attend a premiere and its after party."

"Oh, duh," she says. "Of course I'm excited about that too."

I laugh, and she reaches over and turns up the music. And it's like we're teenagers again, cruising the loop around town for fun.

A few hours later and we're being escorted out of LAX to the car I have waiting to take us to my apartment. Thankfully, I hadn't gotten rid of it yet. I was living with Paul mostly, but I kept the apartment just in case. It was like I knew things weren't going to last. If only I'd listen to my intuition more often.

My apartment is a quaint studio on Hollywood Boulevard. I moved in shortly after I got the role for the movie. It was close enough to Paul and close enough to the studio where most of the in-studio scenes were shot.

When we pull up to the front, Evan is in awe. "Oh, this is nice."

"Wait until you see the inside. It's awesome," I tell her. "My apartment is small, but it's all I needed at the time and was in my budget. Plus, it has full-time security, which is always nice, because people are always coming through this area to see if they can spot a celebrity or two."

"That must get annoying," Evan shudders.

"I haven't fully experienced it yet, except that time someone photographed me at Chipotle the day the news broke that I was the star in the film." I cringe. That was weird.

"Oh, I saw that. Archer bought like every copy at our grocery store so no one else could see it."

I laugh. "That's such an Archer thing to do."

"It totally is."

When we finally get to the door of my apartment, I pull my key out and unlock the door. Everything is just as I left it. Pictures of me, Archer, and Evan are sprinkled throughout. Paul hated pictures of Ace, but I didn't care. He's my best friend, and not even Paul was going to come between us.

There are also pictures of me and my parents. And some eclectic art things I've bought at various art walks the city puts on.

We turn the corner to see the completely open room that includes a kitchen with gray and natural wood cabinets and top-of-the-line appliances, an eat-in dining table, and a super cute gray sofa with funky pillows I found on sale at a furniture store.

Across from the sofa, there's a door leading to a full bathroom with a shower and tub and stackable washer and dryer set. Next to that is my queen-sized bed, decorated in gray neutrals and more funky pillows to complete the space.

"This is a really adorable place, Bay," she says, looking around, taking it all in.

"Thank you." I need to pee, so I excuse myself quickly to go to the bathroom.

When I'm done, Evan is waiting to go herself.

We sit on the sofa and relax a little after the flight and car ride here and both end up falling asleep. A little cat nap never hurt anyone.

Before long, my alarm starts going off, letting me know we need to wake up and get to the dinner reservations I made on the car ride home.

I picked the cutest little Greek restaurant a block from here, so we don't have to worry about driving or getting a car to get us anywhere.

Once we order, Evan strikes up a conversation with the table next to us. They're not really thrilled about it, because people here just aren't used to East Texas charm.

They cut her off and get back to eating their dinner quickly before she can suck them in with another conversation. "Wow, rude," she says, and I laugh so hard soda dribbles out of my mouth a little. I manage to hold the rest in and swallow.

"Don't make me laugh when I'm taking a drink," I tell her, still laughing.

"Whoops. My bad."

After dinner, we stroll around the Walk of Fame, and I point out the famous people I've worked with so far. She seems super impressed. "Oh, there's Julie Andrews! I love her." There are hundreds and hundreds of them, too many for us to see in one night, so we make our way back to my apartment, where we promptly change into pajamas and crash.

The next day is premiere day, so it's a complete day of pampering. I booked us an appointment for nails, hair, and makeup.

Evan is super excited, and she even found a beautiful dress on sale at the mall.

My dress is a one-shoulder, dual-tone organza dress. A pretty deep-maroon and black. I absolutely adore it.

We both get nail colors to complement our dresses.

For hair, I go with a straight, sleek look that comes around and sits on my shoulder with a small braid. Evan goes with a curly look, with it pulled back slightly in fishbone braiding. She looks absolutely stunning.

When we are done being pampered, the limo the studio got for me and my plus-one arrives at my apartment. It's decked out with a full bar, which I was told I needed to take advantage of to settle some nerves.

"Oooh," Evan says when she sees the bar. "So it looks like we have tequila, vodka, gin, rum, and scotch. I think I'm going to go with tequila. What's your poison?"

"What brand is the vodka?" I ask.

She pulls it out of the area it's strapped down to. "Oh, it looks like it's Tito's."

"Oh, sweet. They actually listened to my request." That's awesome. "I'll take the Tito's with Sprite, please."

Evan downs her tequila in one shot before pouring a good helping of vodka with a splash of Sprite. I roll my eyes at her but take the drink anyway.

"What?" she asks. "You said the ride would be

short, so I figured the best way to get your nerves calm is plenty of vodka for you to down quickly."

I shrug. She's not wrong, so I drink it as fast as I can, and when I'm done, the driver announces we're third in line to be dropped off. One of the red-carpet coordinators jumps in—like I expected but forgot to tell Evan about, so she jumps, terrified, thinking we're being robbed, and goes into action mode.

"Wait, stop, this is the red-carpet coordinator. She's going to tell us what to do."

"Oh, sorry." Evan backs down and listens closely to what she tells us.

"So, Bayleigh, you two are going to be dropped off in two more stops. You will both get out and begin the interview tour." Evan and I both nod. She's nervous. I've done the red carpet before, but never to this scale, so I'm trying to remember all my media training so I don't screw this up.

The lady looks down at her sheet and sees that my plus-one isn't listed, but I'm entitled to one, so she glances over and asks, "What's your name?"

"Evan Scott," she says before spelling it out for her, and the lady shoots a text off to someone, I assume to update my plus-one on the guest list.

"Okay, so we're up. Evan, you're going to be getting out with her, but stay behind. You're her support system at this thing. Let her answer questions, then move on to the next interviewer."

We both nod and Evan grabs my hand. It's clammy, but I'm trying not to show my nervousness.

"All right, here you two go." She pushes me out first, and the crowd cheers, then Evan exits as the crowd continues to shout, and we're ushered through the line of media people.

I'm asked to pose and answer questions about my role in the movie and how I liked working with my costars. I give all the media-approved answers before finally getting inside to our seats, between my agent and one of my costars.

The excitement in the room is palpable as the director comes out and thanks us for a job well done before the movie starts.

A couple of hours later and we're exiting the room. "Wow," Evan says. "That was fucking awesome."

"Yeah?" I ask, unsure. It's still so weird seeing myself on a screen.

"Hell yeah, I'm sure," she answers honestly.

"So…" I click my tongue. "I'm really tired and not feeling the after-party. Would it hurt your feelings if we didn't go?" I also know there's usually a ton of drugs and stuff at those things, and I'm just not feeling all that tonight. But if Evan wants to go to experience it, we'll do it.

She yawns. "Yeah, I'm exhausted. I'm game to just go back to your apartment and sleep." She looks at her watch. "Oh yeah, it's like four in the morning back home. No wonder we're so tired."

"Yup, that jetlag is awful. I promise we'll go do all your touristy stuff tomorrow, and I have a meeting with my agent the next day before we head back to Texas."

"Sounds good," she says.

I'm thankful. I'm not in a partying mood tonight.

As much as I was looking forward to this and am glad Evan is getting to experience it, the one person I want the most isn't here. He had just taken ten days off work for me to go on my non-honeymoon, so I couldn't ask him to take another week off and put his dad in a bind that close together.

Plus… I'm still not sure where we stand.

Are we just fuck buddies now? Friends with benefits? Are we more?

God, I hope we're more.

TWENTY-ONE

NUMB

Archer

Pissed. Aggravated. Frustrated. Heartbroken.

All the emotions are flying through me right now.

I don't know why I let myself get involved with someone so unavailable. Well, yeah, I do.

Bayleigh and Evan jetted off to L.A. a couple of days ago, and who knows when I will see Bayleigh again. There's not a future for us. Never was.

She fucked me and left.

I feel like such a fucking girl right now.

It's Saturday, which means the clinic is closed to-day, and I'm actually really pissed off about that too. At least work would get my mind off things.

I decide to throw on my gray jogging pants and tennis shoes to run. The wieners get excited, because they think we're going for a quick walk, but their little legs can't handle what I need right now. "No, girls, not today." I reach down and pet both of them gently on the heads and rub their bellies before tossing them each a treat, grabbing my water bottle, and heading out the door.

After sticking my headphones in my ears and starting my running playlist, I take off on my usual jog.

Why did I let myself get involved with her that way? It was more than us just being drunk. I wanted it—and so did she.

Was it worth it? I have no fucking idea.

I never really thought of us being together in that way before the trip.

Will we ever be the same? Hell no. I don't even know if I can look at her as a friend again.

We're at an impasse. I can't leave Sunnyville, and she's too bright of a star to keep smothered in small-town East Texas. I wouldn't ever ask her to give up her dream for me, just like I know she wouldn't ask me to leave my family and business behind.

My dad is getting older and ready to retire soon. My life has been planned out for me since day one. And while that sounds awful, it's not. I truly love what I do. And I wouldn't do that to my parents. I couldn't. She wouldn't ask that of me, would she?

What the hell am I thinking? We never even talked about next steps like that. Maybe I was just a "hit it and quit it" for her. *Goddammit.*

By this point, I'm at a full sprint on a backroad that goes out by one of the bigger farms in the area. I slow down and put my hands on my head to normalize my breathing before chugging some water and picking my pace back up.

When I do, I allow myself to think about the what ifs.

What if she decided she didn't like acting? Would she come back home and live out a quiet life in Sunnyville?

What if I decided to up and move to L.A. to be with her for her career? Would I start up a clinic there or get a job at one that sees celebrities' pets? I cringe at that thought. I much prefer cows and horses to celebrities. Maybe I'd just be a kept man. I basically gag at that thought. No. I could never just be a kept man.

It's just not a possibility.

I need to let Bayleigh go.

I need to get her out of my system.

And pray that one day we can at least be friends again.

Friends, when both of us have moved on. Not likely. I'll be ready to punch whatever dude she decides to marry. Probably some big-shot actor. She'll probably have beautiful babies with him and everything.

An even more cringy thought.

I need to get my mind off Bayleigh and our not-possible-future together.

I run past Mr. Bill's farm and see the cows lying in the grass with the new calf we delivered the other day. The one that was breech. They're doing well, and that's so good to see.

Life goes on.

Life fucking goes on.

When I finally make it back to my house, Liv is sitting out on the front porch with lemonade, always with the lemonade. "Archer!" she yells.

I wave.

"Get over here and get you a drink."

I can't say no to her, so I jog over and grab the glass she pours for me. "Thank you, Mrs. Hart," I say as I start chugging the refreshing liquid.

"Stop it," she admonishes. "You've grown up now. Please, call me Liv."

"Yes, ma'am." I smile as I finish the lemonade and hand her back the empty glass. "Thank you."

"Would you like some more?"

"No, thank you. I better get home and shower." I take a step back, hoping she doesn't force the issue. I really don't feel like having a conversation with the mother of the woman I'm in love with.

"Oh, all right, dear." She smiles, and before she can

say anything else, I finish the jog back home.

A few minutes later, I'm in my bathroom, peeling off the sweaty clothes sticking to my body and turning on the shower.

While I wait for the water to warm, I pick up my phone and open up a social media app. Not sure why I expected anything different, but Evan's profile pops up first with selfies of her and Bayleigh exploring L.A.

Looks like Bayleigh is taking her all over the city. Evan has never been to California, but she fits right in.

Pictures of them with the iconic Hollywood sign behind them, on Hollywood Boulevard, and on some famous peoples' stars. I'm glad Evan is having the time of her life. I'm thankful Bayleigh found her place in the world—even if it's not with me.

I close out the app and set my phone back down on the counter before jumping in the shower. I sit under the hot tap for what feels like forever. It's too hot, but it feels good.

As much as I try not to let it, my mind wanders to Bayleigh. I think back to the morning I woke up with my hand on her breast. And how I wish we could wake up like that every morning.

I think back to the first night we had sex—even drunk, it was some of the most explosive sex I've ever had.

Then a couple of nights ago, when neither of us could resist each other.

And then she left.

Barely said anything but "thanks."

Fucking "thanks."

Are you kidding me?

Now, I'm fucking pissed again.

My phone dings with a text. I pick it up and see it's my sister sending an attachment.

Evan: BIG BRO!!!! It's so pretty here. Wish you were with us. I think Bayleigh wishes that too.

It's an image of the two of them on top of one of those double-decker Los Angeles buses they use for the tours around the city. Evan with huge-ass sunglasses and a hat she's having to hold on to so it doesn't fly off. Bayleigh looking as beautiful as ever, but with a brown wig on, I assume to hide her identity, but I love her blonde.

Me: Ha, thanks, but no thanks. L.A. is not for me. Glad you're having fun, baby sis.

Evan: Party pooper. (crazy face emoji)

I decide not to reply. I truly am glad she's having fun, but I'm jealous she's with Bayleigh. And pissed our life has turned out like this.

I decide I need a night out of my house, so I open a new text thread and message my friend Rhett. He's some super-smart dork that works in a lab doing God knows what. Probably making bombs or something for the government.

Me: Hey, dude, got any plans tonight?

Rhett: Nope.

Me: Wanna hit up the clubs in Shreveport?

Rhett: Hell yeah. I'll be at your house in an hour.

Me: Sounds good, bro.

At that, I go to my closet and pick out my nicest pair of jeans, a button-down shirt, and the cleanest pair of boots I own.

An hour later, Rhett is knocking on my door, wild and ready to go. "Yo, man, what's up?"

We grab each other's hand and bro-hug. "Nothing much, just bored and needed a night out."

"Fine with me. Been a rough few months at work." He laughs.

"Ahh... making bombs can't be that taxing, dude," I joke.

"Well... it is if you accidently set one off, fucker," he jokes back. He really doesn't make bombs, but we all know what he does is some highly classified thing for the government, so who actually fucking knows.

The forty-minute ride is uneventful. Rhett kept the music pretty loud, so we didn't talk much.

When we walk into The Alamo, a small country bar,

one of our favorites in the "big" city, we find two empty stools next to each other. The bartender spots us immediately. "Hey, guys, what'll it be for ya tonight?"

"I'll have a Jack and coke," I reply immediately, and Rhett says, "I'll have the same."

The DJ is playing a popular country song, and there's a group of people line dancing on the dance floor.

"Go out there, Arch." Rhett nudges me.

"Nah, gonna just drink and people-watch," I say.

"Fine, I'mma go show some ladies how well I can two-step." He laughs, then saunters off to the dance floor.

I hand my card to the bartender and tell him to keep a tab open.

Rhett finds some single lady on the dance floor, and he's spinning her around like he owns every inch of her. She's loving every second of it.

That used to be me. We'd come here, and I'd show all the ladies my dance moves. I can shake it like the best of 'em. On the dance floor and in the bedroom.

I finish off my drink and turn around to signal for another, when I feel a tap on my shoulder. It's Rhett with the girl he was dancing with and another girl, her friend, I guess.

"Archer!" he yells over the music. "This here is Candy and her friend Tiffany." He motions to the other girl. "Come dance with us." He winks.

I throw back the drink Rhett ordered but didn't

drink, then stand up to go dance with Tiffany.

When we make it to the dance floor, the song switches to one of my favorites '90s country songs that's perfect to dance to. I look at Tiffany. "You know how to two-step?" She nods, and we get into an almost perfect rhythm.

Never perfect though—only Bayleigh could ever fully dance with me. In high school, we always caught people's attention when we would swing dance. Not many people can do it anymore, but we perfected it one year for a school talent show, and it just stuck.

I'm spinning Tiffany around the dance floor when the song morphs into a slow one for us to catch our breath. We stand there and sway for a bit when she gets on her tiptoes and comes in for a kiss.

My gut instinct is to tell her no, but what do they say... the best way to get over someone is to get under someone else?

So I kiss her.

Instinctively, my eyes close, and I get lost for a second.

Images of Bayleigh flash in my mind.

Her asking me to kiss her.

Me pushing her up against the wall at her mom's that night.

Her under me.

I back away from the woman in my arms.

Fuuuck.

"What's wrong?"

Shit. I guess I said that out loud. "Ummm… nothing. I just can't be here."

I turn and tap Rhett on the shoulder and tell him I'm going to close out the tab.

"What the fuck, dude? We've only been here an hour." He's pissed. And trying to get laid.

"I know. I just can't do it tonight."

"Fuck. Messing with my mojo here."

The girl he's with—Candy, I think—walks away when Tiffany motions that they need to find some other dudes to sink their teeth into.

"Sorry," I apologize to Rhett. "I'm just not feeling it tonight. I thought I was."

"Well, here." He hands me his keys. "Head back home, and I'll get a ride back from a buddy who lives in town."

I nod and turn to head out.

I don't know what I was thinking. I knew coming here Rhett was going to try to pick up chicks. It's what we used to do back in our college days.

I guess I thought some piece of me could do it, but I'm not that guy anymore. As much as I want to be. As much as I want to forget about Bay. I can't.

When I'm back home, I pour myself some whiskey and drink until I'm numb.

Numb and alone. Probably how I'll end up if I can't have Bayleigh Hart.

My phone buzzes, signifying a phone call. It's my sister. She's still in L.A. with Bayleigh, and it's not like her to call—she usually texts—so I answer it. "Hey, sis."

"Hey, big bro," she starts in a way-too-happy voice. "Whatcha doin'?"

"Nothin' much," I answer honestly.

"Good, so you're not around anyone?" she questions, and I'm afraid to know where her line of questioning is going.

She and Bayleigh could be up to anything. Bay is bad, but Evan is worse. Fuck me, she's not calling from jail, is she? I take a quick look at my phone to confirm that it's her phone she's calling from and breathe out a sigh of relief. I'm working my way out from some pretty heavy student loans, and bail for two could put a crimp in those plans.

"No, home alone," I answer her question.

There's silence on the other end of the line for a hot second. "Coool," she drawls and clicks her tongue. I wait rather than jump into what she's wanting. I know whatever she's about to ask me that I do not want to answer. My palms start sweating, and my hairline tingles in that weird way that tells you something bad is about to happen. And my gut cramps like I ate a bad bucket of shrimp, so something bad is clearly about to come out of her mouth. She doesn't know, does she? She couldn't. Bay wouldn't tell her. That's private. I haven't told anyone, and Bayleigh wouldn't either. "Sooo... what happened between you and Bayleigh?"

Fuck. I knew that's where this was going. "Nothing, why?" I lie. Maybe she's just fishing. Bayleigh didn't tell her shit. She wouldn't. She just wants it all to go away so she can go on with her life in Hollywood. I was nothing more than a vacation fling. And that cuts fucking deep, because somewhere along the way, Bayleigh became more. She became everything.

"Well, it's just that both of you have been off since y'all got back, and it's been kind of..." She trails off, and like a fucking car crash I know is coming, I ask the one question I fucking know I shouldn't.

"Kind of what?"

"Uncomfortable," she answers.

"Nothing happened!" I shout, and even I wince at my tone. I'm way too defensive off the bat. When we were kids, I always got in trouble because I was a shit liar. I still am, and I don't consider it a bad thing usually, but when I'm trying to hide my shattered pride and broken heart, it's kind of a pain in the fucking ass.

"I'm not buying that, Arch," Evan replies. She of course sees right through me; she always has. I was wrong, little sisters aren't kind of a pain in the ass, they're always a pain in the ass like that. We've always been close. We're less than two years apart and never really fought growing up like our friends' and their sib-lings did. She's always been one of my best friends. So of course she doesn't believe me.

"I'm telling you, nothing fucking happened." I'm calmer this time but still frustrated I'm having to go through this line of questioning. To divert the topic off me, I ask, "What are y'all up to?"

"Bayleigh is in a meeting with her agent. Apparently, she's got two parts lined up, but she has to choose one," Evan answers, and it hits me like a rock in my gut. I knew it was going to happen, but still, I should have anticipated it. And even though I knew it was coming, it still fucking hurts.

Go fucking figure. We all knew she'd be a big star. We knew she was too bright for Sunnyville. I'm the one who went and caught fucking feelings for a girl I can never have.

"That's awesome." I take a deep breath and run my hands through my hair. "We always knew she would go far." I try to sound sincere. I hope she buys it. And the part that shits me is I would never want to hold her back. It's why she can never know that somewhere on her not-honeymoon, I fell in love with her. I can't hold her back. It would kill me if I did.

"Yup, we did, but the thing is…" She pauses, and it sounds like she takes a sip out of a straw. I roll my eyes. Only Evan would drink a damn fountain soda instead of imparting important wisdom on me.

"The thing is?" I prompt, hoping she'll hurry the fuck along this painful conversation.

"She didn't seem happy or excited going into that meeting," Evan finishes.

"Okaaay…."

"She seemed very conflicted. Almost like one or both decisions will break her in some way," she confides. "I think she's really torn."

"They're both probably huge parts, sis," I reply. And they probably are. She needs to choose whichever will be the better career move for her. After landing this last role, she's right on the cusp and needs to be smart about what she signs on for. "She's probably talking out which one will be the bigger hit right now."

"No, I don't think that's it," she says, and I hear another slurp through her straw as she takes a sip of whatever she's drinking. "I think it's got to do with some life decisions. And I am almost positive you're the reason she's suddenly not happy here."

"Wait, what?" I ask. She's not happy in L.A.? That's interesting. The last time we talked before the wedding, she loved her life there. "What do you mean?" I realize I shouldn't have asked, because it's going to tip her off that something *did* happen.

"Well, she kept saying she misses home and that L.A. just isn't where she wants to be anymore, but she also loves her job and doesn't know what to do."

Before I can reply, I hear a woman's high-pitched

voice in the background. "I think you're making a serious mistake, Bayleigh."

"Gotta go, Arch. I'll talk to you later." Evan hangs up before I can reply, and that's the end of that.

My mind starts wandering. What mistake could she be making?

TWENTY-TWO

Bayleigh

"I've made up my mind," I say as I turn the keys to unlock the front door of my apartment.

My agent chases me all the way from the conference room. She doesn't agree with me, but I don't care.

"I think you're making a serious mistake, Bayleigh!" she shrieks as I step into the lobby, and she follows me inside, pushing the door open before it can close. Since when is she such a shrieker? It's annoying as fuck.

"Gotta go, Arch. I'll talk to you later," Evan says as she drops the hand holding her cell phone and presses the little red circle to end her call.

I want to ask her what they were talking about or how he's doing. Did he sound like he missed me? But then she would know I didn't just sleep with her brother on vacation; I fell in love with him. Truthfully, I've always been in love with him and have since he punched Bobby Guthrie in the nose when he pulled the heads off all my Barbie dolls. Bobby had it coming, but after that, I knew Archer was the one. I thought he'd come around.

Spoiler alert: he never did.

And then I saw his penis and learned first-hand what he could do with it. Sure, it was awkward as hell, and we easily could have let it push us apart, but I'm nothing if not a determined woman. I finally got a glimpse of what my life would be like with Archer in a starring role, and I'm not giving it up without a fight.

"I said I've made up my mind."

"But a television show?" she asks. "Those are big movies that want you to sign on."

"I know they are," I reply. "So big that they'd film for months, then promote for more months, then off to another location to shoot."

"I know!" she says excitedly. "Isn't it great?"

"It is," I agree. "But what if I want more?"

"More?" my agent asks. "Honey, I can get you more money. Why didn't you say something?"

"I don't want more money," I explain and look at Evan, who's following this conversation with her head flipping back and forth like she's watching the toughest match at Wimbledon. She holds her two thumbs-up to me with a wide smile on her face in encouragement.

"Well, then what do you want?" she asks me.

"More to life."

"Is this about Paul?" she asks, and Evan frowns.

"No," I answer, looking back to my agent. "Not really. He's an ass. It's more about the life I want. A life he could never give me."

"What does that mean?"

"It means I want to be near my family for some of the year," I say before taking a deep breath and continuing. "I want to watch the high school team win state. I want to get a puppy."

"So get a puppy. Paris Hilton has a puppy!" she shouts, clearly exasperated.

"I want to get married to a man who really loves me, one I really love, and have a baby," I say, and my agent gasps. "Not now, but eventually."

"Good, because your career is just taking off."

"I know that," I tell her gently.

"And you think this show can do that?" she asks.

"I do. I think it'll allow me the balance I need in my life before I finally snap and shave myself bald before smashing in the windows of Paul's Ferrari in front of a bunch of snap-happy paparazzi."

"God, don't even say that out loud." She shudders before moving on. "Well, streaming is the next big thing."

"It just might be," I reply with a smile, knowing she's coming around to my way of thinking.

"Well," she says as she looks me over. "I'll go finalize the contracts."

"Thank you."

"What are you going to do?" she asks. "You have a little bit of a break before awards season and the pilot shoots."

"I'm going home to Texas."

"And what will you do there?" Evan has a twinkle in her eye and I know in my gut that even if neither of us ever told her outright that something happened in Bora Bora, Evan is a crafty enough bitch to figure it out herself. I'd be impressed if I wasn't the one who's life dramas were rolled out in front of everyone like a bad dick pic right now. One day the tables will be turned and I'm going to enjoy the hell out of it.

It's time to make a decision. It's time to be a good Texas girl and take a stand.

"I'm gonna go get my man."

"Hell yes, bitch!" Evan shouts, and my agent just laughs before mouthing her wish for me to just be happy.

And for the first time in a long time, I think I just might be.

TWENTY-THREE

CAN'T BE HERE

Archer

Nelly's "Hot in Herre" sounds through the room, and I open my eyes. It's my favorite song and has been ever since Hannah Montgomery stripped to it while dancing with me at Grad Night. *Ahhh, memories.* And those are the kind that stick with a teenage boy's mind even after he's made it to a respectable adulthood. I slide my finger across the screen to answer.

"Hello," I answer.

"Oh, I'm sorry. Did I wake you?" My mom seems only slightly concerned. I look at the time and realize I slept in way too late. Usually, I would have been up; I'd have already gotten a workout in, showered, and finishing a smoothie by now. Last night was different. I'd decided to let my feelings get the better of me. With Bayleigh and Evan living their best celebrity life in California, I decided to have a guys' night with my old friends *Johnny* and *Walker*. It wasn't my finest moment, but it got the job done. Nothing like making yourself absolutely miserable so you can do nothing the next day but move on, and the hangover you got as a parting gift serves as a memory of why you should never go back.

"Yeah, but it's okay. I need to get up anyway." I sit up, stretch, and hope I don't throw up on the carpet. I really like this carpet, and pulling old tack strips sucks.

"Evan gets back home tonight, so I'm cooking dinner. I want to hear all about her trip to L.A.!" She pauses for a moment and then adds almost as an afterthought, "You should come."

Awesome. Even my own family loves Bayleigh more than me. It figures they'd choose her over me. Not that they know there was anything to choose anyone over, but still. It fucking stings. And I'm not even sure she's coming back to Texas in the end. Her life is just taking off now, she doesn't need to come here and be surrounded with nothing but rolling hills and time. She needs to spread her wings. And as much as I want to keep her, I don't think it's the right thing *for her.*

I mentally cringe. I don't want to hear about the trip my sister took with Bayleigh. A night full of all the famous people Evan rubbed elbows with and how awesome California is. And worst of all, how Bayleigh is never coming back. I knew it would shake down like that. I really did, and I'm happy for her and so fucking proud, but dammit, I'm going to miss that girl and all her crazy blonde curls and wild ideas she cooks up with my sister.

"Bayleigh will be there," she says, and I cuss. Why? Why is Bayleigh coming back home? I still don't want to go. But I do. As much as I need to move on from this bullshit, I need to see her more. "Archer?"

"I'll be there, Mom." I sigh. I've never missed a family meal, and I don't intend to start now. It would be suspicious if I did. I'm fucking pathetic. I guess I'll just have to deal with it.

I spend the rest of the day going back and forth fighting internally with myself—half of me wanting to cancel, because I don't want to listen to all the stuff Evan got to do with Bayleigh, and the other half not wanting to disappoint my mom. I shouldn't go, but there's something inside me that won't let me *not* go.

Disappointing my mom is the last thing I ever want to do. I'll go eat quickly, then say I'm not feeling well or something and bow out early. Or maybe I'll hit Taco Bell on the way home. Nothing like a little hair of the dog and Satan's snack sack to burn a hangover out of the gut. Sounds like a solid plan to me.

The last few days were so mundane they just bled

together, one right after another. Busy days at work and squeezing run times in. That's about it.

It's when my head hit my pillow that I really wanted and needed sleep, but it never came. No matter how hard I try, I cannot get my mind off Bayleigh. And it pisses me the fuck off. I want—no, I *need*—to move on. It's the only way I'm going to find some semblance of a way to be okay. Whining and mooning have never been my style, so I got up and grabbed the bottle and took it out back to stare at the stars.

Bayleigh and I were meant to be friends and nothing more.

After coming to peace with all the heavy thoughts swirling around in my brain and bourbon in my belly, I headed to bed and finally found sleep, even if my heart hurt.

I drive up to my parents' house. This was the house my grandparents lived in when Evan and I were kids and I live in the house we grew up in now. This is a colonial-style built in the early 1900s out in the country on a fair bit of land. It's a family home for us. My great-grandparents bought it and handed it down to my grand-father, then my parents. My parents completely gutted it when they moved in about thirty years ago, right after they were married. It was when my grandfather retired, and he and my grandmother wanted to travel the world in a Winnebago. And they sure had fun. My parents built a full wing on the house for when they were done with their adventures. That's where they live now. It's the perfect arrangement.

I walk into the house, and I'm greeted by the smell of my mom's cooking. It smells like her famous pot roast. Mine and Evan's favorite meal. "Mom, Dad, I'm here."

"In the kitchen!" my mom yells back, and I make my way toward the back of the house where the kitchen is. She's facing away from me at the sink, cleaning some dishes before the rest of the guests arrive.

"Hey, Mom," I say when I'm at the center island.

"Oh hey, Arch," she says as she walks over to give me a quick hug without touching me with her hands. "Sorry, hands are wet."

We both laugh. "No worries, Mom. I see you cooked my favorite." I smile.

"Evan's too. And Bayleigh's." She smiles as I try to hide my nervousness of seeing her again. "Remember when Bayleigh would come over for dinner because she heard it was roast night?" I nod. "You three could put down an entire roast. I had to start doubling my recipe so your father had plenty to eat too."

"We sure did. It's so good. I hope you made extra tonight too. I'm starving," I say, patting my stomach.

"I did." She turns back to finish washing one of the pots she used. "Oh, will you set the table real fast? We need seven."

"Who all is coming?" I already know the answer,

but I'm hoping it's different from what I'm thinking.

"Well, me, your dad, your grandparents, you, Evan, and Bayleigh," she says, putting a finger up for each person she counts. "Yeah, seven."

"Okay," I reply and grab the plates and silverware to put on the dining room table.

I still don't know why is Bayleigh coming back home? Maybe she had more of a break before her next project. I'm trying not to be frustrated. I need distance between us, and her sitting at the same table as me in *my* family's home is *not* distance.

Before I can dwell any longer, I hear the front door open and my sister scream out, "Honey, I'm home!" I roll my eyes. Evan is a handful, to say the least. One day, she's going to find a man she can steam roll and put his balls right in her old lady pocketbook. Just like Granny's. Poor fucker. At least then I'll have someone to sympathize with. Or get drunk and watch a game with.

"Ahhh!" my mom screams and runs to the door to hug her like she's been gone for years or something. I roll my eyes—always the favorite kid. "How was it? Tell me everything!"

"Let's eat first, Mom. We're starving. Airport food sucks. I smell pot roast." Before my mom can reply, Evan has made her way into the kitchen that connects to the dining room. "Hey, Arch." She walks over and gives me a huge bear hug.

"Hey, sis." I hug her back.

"Well, don't you just look like hammered horse shit," my grandpa says when he walks in the room.

"Tom!" my grandma scolds. "You can't say shit like that."

"Really?" he asks. "I just did."

"Jesus H.," she grumbles before turning to me. "You look just… fine, honey. Just fine."

"She's as full of shit as a Christmas goose," he practically shouts. "You look like shit. What happened?"

"Fucking Christ!" Grandma snaps. "Stop saying 'shit' so fucking much."

"But good God damn, I love that woman," he says with a twinkle in his eye.

I can't help it. I laugh. I love Grandpa. He did some crazy shit in Vietnam and slowed down to be a drill instructor like the one in *Full Metal Jacket*. He's the best guy I know. And who I call when I need help pulling a calf, because he's so damn stubborn he'll never give up.

"I'm all right." I answer cryptically, "Or I will be."

"Good man," he says quietly as he pats me on the shoulder. "If not, I have a flask in my coat pocket. Nothing says 'time heals all wounds' quite like tequila."

"Thanks, Grandpa." I laugh even as my belly burns at the thought of adding tequila on top of the bourbon that still hasn't completely made it through my system yet. Grandpa, who is kind of an asshole—a loveable asshole, but still an asshole—knows exactly what he's doing, because he chuckles at my wince and pats his breast pocket as he walks by, that wily old fucker.

Suddenly, I hear Mom talking to Bayleigh, but I can't make out what they're saying. She sounds overly excited about something though. Probably that big movie role she signed on to. I inwardly shrug and walk back toward the restroom to wash my hands. I purposefully take the route through the house to avoid seeing Bayleigh.

When I walk out of the restroom, I hear Mom call, "Archer, time to eat."

When I get to the dining room, the food is set up on the table, family buffet style, and everyone is already seated. I walk over to where my grandparents are sitting, trying to grab a seat with them. They both smile at me—Grandma sweetly, but Grandpa just grins ear-to-ear—before I look around to find the open seat… right next to Bayleigh. Of course it is.

It's like a sock to the gut. Like the time Toby Abbott hit me for staring at Gina Conrad's ass in her cheer uniform in the tenth grade. I had no idea they'd been secretly dating for a week and besides, everyone knew she didn't wear panties under the little skirt. It's like too much whiskey on an empty stomach.

I should have known he was up to something. He pats his pocket again and snickers as I shake my head and probably turn a few shades of green—whether at the prospect of more alcohol or a closer proximity to the one woman I've ever really loved and can't have, I don't know.

"Hey, Ace." Bayleigh smiles like we're back to being just friends, and it burns deep in my gut with yesterday's bourbon.

"Hey," I say probably a little too curtly and take my seat just before my dad starts the traditional dinner prayer. I hate feeling trapped, like I don't have any choices. And before Bora Bora, my family saving me the seat next to Bayleigh would have been a welcome sight, but now it's just another reminder of what I can't have. I feel like I'm starting to sound like a spoiled child, and I hate that. I need to accept that life has backed me into a corner, and I'll figure my way out of it later. But for now, I need to eat this dinner my mother has made.

"All right, y'all, settle down so I can bless the food," my dad says in his deep baritone, I-mean-business voice. "*Thank you, Lord, for this food, and bless the cans that hand it.*"

It makes me smile every time. It was a funny slip-up years ago, and it's stuck ever since. Short, sweet, and to the point, but with the word flip. It does a fair amount to shake me out of the shitty mood I was headed toward a moment ago.

"Everybody, dig in," my mom says, grabbing the mashed potatoes to scoop some on her plate while I grab a roll and pass the napkin-covered basket to Bayleigh.

"Thank you," Bay says as she takes it from my hand

to grab her own and pass it around.

The passing of the dishes continues until everyone has everything they want and their plates are filled to the brim. When I was a kid and we all met for Sunday dinner at Granny and Grandpa's, this was the norm, and it hasn't changed since my mom took the torch when my grandma couldn't do it all anymore. It's one of the constants I've looked forward to my entire life.

My mom, ready to hear more about their trip, pipes up. "Tell us all about L.A., Evan." She's practically bouncing in her seat, and if she did little clappy hands right now, I wouldn't be surprised. She's that excited. I have no idea why. What I do know is my mom is one of my favorite people on the planet, so if she wanted to go shop Rodeo Drive and put her feet over John Wayne's in cement, I'd book a flight tomorrow to take her, so I sit back and enjoy her enthusiasm with a smile on my face.

Evan goes on and on about all the things they did in "Hell Hole Hollywood," as she calls it. My sister has always been happy right here, where we're from. The place any chance I had with Bayleigh goes to die—or at least that's what I call it in my head.

I tune out everyone talking and just eat Mom's roast, but it's just not the same tonight. Everything tastes sour because of the literal sour taste I have in my mouth over having to listen to this bullshit. Or the Johnny Walker Black. Who knows? I just don't *fucking* care. Not any-more. I smile and nod, but in truth, I'm not really listening. Hell, I'm not *really* even in the room.

"Archer." My dad is talking to me. I'm pretty sure he's said my name more than once. Oops. I probably should have been paying at least a little bit of attention.

"Yeah," I answer quickly.

"There's another cow with a breech calf. Mr. Bill has asked one of us to come out and help. You up for it?"

"Oh, I got it, Dad." I start getting up from my spot at the table. This is the perfect out. Thank God for small favors. "You stay and enjoy dinner."

"You sure, son? I can come help." He begins standing too, but I can tell he wants to stay, and I'm perfectly capable of doing it by myself. And I really need away from Bayleigh and Evan's California lovefest. I swear I heard Evan say she would move there in a heartbeat. And that's a hell fucking no. I won't lose the love of my life *and* my sister to that fucking place.

"Yeah, Dad. Sit down and eat," I reply as I get up. I run and hug my mom and sister before shouting, "Bye, everyone. See y'all later." I sneak a glance at Bayleigh, and she looks like she's about to cry. It hurts to see the pain slash across her face, although I have no idea why. She's the one who hit it and quit it—twice. I made it perfectly clear I would always want her, didn't I?

Before I can do or say anything else, I run out the door to deliver this calf. Anything is better than being in the same room as Bayleigh Hart right now. Because my heart feels like Mike Tyson took it to the mat, and I'm not sure I could survive another round.

TWENTY-FOUR

WHAT THE...

Bayleigh

"Bye, everyone. See y'all later," Archer says as he runs out the door.

What the…? What the fuck was that? I look over at Evan, and she seems just as shocked as I do, but everyone else is going about their daily business as if Archer just didn't give me the cold shoulder throughout dinner. He barely even looked at me once. He just kept shoveling pot roast into his mouth like it was his job. To be fair, it's a great fucking pot roast that I happen to know magically comes from two packets of au jus, two packets of ranch mix, a stick of butter, and a small jar of banana peppers. There is not one thing healthy about it, but it's freaking delicious. But still… he didn't even say hi.

I was planning on telling Archer tonight about me moving back home to Sunnyville.

Netflix is filming a series in Shreveport. One that's supposed to be a pretty long-term gig. Think *True Detective* but grittier and follows a tough-as-nails police detective named Claire. I'm honestly shocked as shit that they even considered me while being overwhelmingly honored at the same time.

It will potentially film eight to nine seasons, and if it does as well as they expect it to, they will continue filming the series there in the future. The contract also leaves four months out of every year open for me to film movie roles, or do crazy things like get married and have a baby—if I can get a groom who wants to stick around, that is. They even said they would potentially write any pregnancies into the script but also aren't opposed to shooting around a belly. They want me so bad they practically offered me anything to sign. So I did. I honestly jumped at the chance, and I did it for Archer and the opportunity to have a life with him. *I did it all for him.*

"What the hell was that?" Evan whispers where only I can hear it. She's sitting right next to me. Archer had been on the other side of me, and he didn't say a single damn word to me.

"I have no idea." I shrug and shake my head. "Excuse me." I place my napkin on the table and get up from the table. I pretend like I'm going to the restroom, but I really need to get out of here before I cry in front of Archer's entire family. To my knowledge, none of them know there's anything between us—that is, unless Evan opened her fat mouth, which is always a possibility. Even when we were kids, she was the biggest tattle-tale. I'm still not entirely sure why we love her so much.

They have no idea I just changed the entire course of my life, and I did it for their son, because I love him that much.

Today was supposed to be a happy day. I was going to get my man back, but my man was cold and distant. And I'm not even sure he's my man. Or that he wants to be.

I barely make it to the door when the tears start to fall. Thankfully, my parents live in the same neighborhood. Once I'm inside, I put the lid down on the toilet, sit down, then put my head in my hands and just let it out as quietly as possible.

I run through the many reasons why Archer could be acting like this. In all the time we've been friends, he's never treated me like this. Never given me the cold shoulder. Of course we fought; who doesn't? Friends have disagreements all the time, and we're no different. But still, we've never held grudges against each other. We've also never gone this long without speaking. Part of that was my fault this past week though. I was working through things while trying to figure out how to live my dream of acting and still be with the person I love the most.

That's when literally the best offer fell into my lap. No, it wouldn't give me recognition like one of the blockbuster films would have, but what it does give me is the best of both worlds. I'm truly okay with not being a huge star. I do want to live out my life without paparazzi always chasing me around. At my core, I'm not a club-hopping party girl. I'm a country girl who drinks whiskey and can pull a calf with the best of them.

I want a family, a house on a farm, and I want it with Archer. I want a whole mess of dark-haired babies and loud barking dogs. I want them to have a childhood where they climb trees and catch frogs, and I want it all right here. I want it with that asshole who just left me at dinner with his family without a backward glance. I realize now that no one else will ever measure up.

So why the treatment tonight?

Is it because I didn't talk to him last week?

The sex did change our relationship. There's no doubt about that at all. It added a layer to it that we both could no longer resist. A delicious layer with orgasms, and everyone knows that orgasms you don't have to give yourself are always awesome.

But what if he doesn't feel the same way?

What if sex actually made him realize he doesn't want me in that way?

I don't know if I can handle that. It took us having sex for me to realize there's no one else in the world for me except for Archer. Hell, I almost married the absolute wrong man because I didn't want to or know how to cope with my feelings for Archer in the first place. The magnitude of what I feel for him was too much, but now I know I should accept nothing less.

Archer is it for me.

I'm pulled out of my thoughts when there's a knock at the door. "Bay?" It's Evan. "You okay?"

"Yeah, I'll be out in a second." I stand and start wiping the tears off my face. I notice there's a box of tissues on the counter, grab one, and look in the mirror. *Shit.* I have mascara running down my face.

"I'm coming in," Evan warns and begins turning the doorknob. I guess I didn't lock it. Crap on a cracker. When the door is open enough she can see my face, she quickly realizes I've been in here crying my eyes out. "Oh, Bay." She pulls me in for a hug, and the tears start to fall again.

"I'm okay. I'm okay." But I'm not. I know it, and she knows it.

Evan reaches around me to grab another tissue before stepping back to help me wipe the tears off my face, *again*. She wipes my mascara from my cheeks and is as gentle as you would be with a child. I wonder if this is how she is with her students. Funny, but I always pictured her more like Grandpa Tom with her kids.

"No, you're not, but you will be."

"Tonight was supposed to be a good night." I sit back down on the toilet lid, and Evan sits on the edge of the bathtub.

"I know," she breathes.

"Why is he acting like this?" I ask.

"How about you tell me what happened on your honeymoon?" Fuck. I can't talk to Archer's sister about this. I'd told her that things had gotten out of hand and that I've been in love with her brother for years when we were drunk on champagne in L.A. but I never gave her the gritty details. "Bayleigh?"

Dammit, well, here it goes. "Well, ummm…" I stammer. "We had—"

She interrupts me before I can continue. "Never mind, I don't want to know. I mean, I thought that might've happened. And that just confirmed it. But he's my brother, and I don't need to know that information."

We both laugh a little. "Hey, you asked."

"I did. I mean, you had pretty much said as much in L.A., but…" She shrugs and moves to the floor in front of me.

"Yeah," I reply sadly.

"Sooo… knowing my big bro, he shuts down when he feels like things aren't going his way."

"What do you mean?"

"You know him just as well as I do, so I'm sure you know this information, but you're blinded by banging."

She cringes at her own words, and I burst out laughing. "Fuck me running. I think I just threw up a little bit."

"Shut up."

"I'm serious," she whines. "I think I'll never be the same again!"

"You're an idiot," I tell her. I do know what she means though. "So this is like that time Archer wanted to be pitcher on the baseball team, but he was much better as the third baseman?"

"Sorta. He wants you, but he also wants you to live out your dream. This was about him wanting what's best for you, even if that's not him. Besides, you both kinda shut down and got awkward with each other when you were back," she says. She slaps my shoulder, then points at me. "And you need to both get your heads out of your asses and fix this shit."

"I know." And I do know. "But… how?"

"He doesn't know you're moving back home for a good long while, does he?"

I shake my head.

"So that could be the fix to all this," she says, but I'm not following. Then again, my eyes are swollen and my nose is stuffy now.

"Huh?"

"Communication, Bayleigh," she says and rolls her eyes at me like I'm an idiot, which I am… until my lightbulb moment.

"Ohhh!" I shout.

Evan does a little dance, then says, "All right, let's get you cleaned up so we don't have to explain to the rest of the family why you've been crying, 'cause if Dad knows Archer is the reason, he will tan his hide."

She reaches into the cabinet above my head for a makeup wipe and starts cleaning the rest of the streaks of mascara off my face. "Thank you," I say, starting to feel better about the situation.

"Welcome, babe." She throws away the wipe, then looks me in the eye. "So now we come up with a game plan."

And we do. One that will get me my man. And the life I've dreamed of. Acting *and* living at home with the love of my life.

TWENTY-FIVE

FIX YOUR SHIT

Archer

The calf didn't make it this time. Rough ones like this are always heartbreaking. The heifers have feelings much like humans. She knew the second we did that the calf was not alive when it finally came out. It was a rough birth.

It took my mind off Bayleigh—for a little while—but now here I am, showering all the cow birth off me, thinking about her again.

I wish things were different, but they aren't. She's going to be a big star, and I'm stuck in Bumfuck, Texas. Never in my life have I wished I were somewhere else. I love it here; truly, I do. But I love Bayleigh more.

Love.

I really don't know when that happened, but go figure it would be with someone I can't have. Someone who deserves more than a fucking small-town vet. Maybe I am nothing but the hick farmer that douchebag Paul likes to call me. I make a decent living and own my own house, but it's nothing compared to the life she will be living in California.

I'm just getting out of the shower when there's a knock at my door, and the dogs are going fucking insane. I quickly dry off, then throw the towel around my waist so I can figure out who's at my damn door.

I see a familiar shape through the opaque glass. It's the one person I don't want to see but want to see all at the same time.

I open it to find Bayleigh, just as beautiful as ever. She looks me up and down, holding back a smile because I'm mostly naked. "Can we... ummm... talk?"

"Sure." I open it wider so she can come in. "Let me put on some clothes."

She nods and comes in. She's suddenly uncomfortable here, and I fucking hate that. I both wish we'd never had sex and am thankful because it was the best sex I've ever had.

I shut the door behind her and make my way into my bedroom, where I pull on a pair of gray sweatpants. When I'm done, I make my way back through the house to find her. She's sitting at my dining room table I rarely use. This is a serious talk, apparently.

I grab the chair across from her and take my seat. "What's up?" I ask, keeping things casual, not knowing where this is going.

"Sooo…" She clicks her tongue. Her nervous habit. It's cute. "I have some news."

I close my eyes and take a deep breath. Knowing where this is going after all. She got a big role and she's leaving me—again. I'm elated and heartbroken all at the same time.

"I.... Well, I had my agent send in some video auditions while we were in Bora Bora. I got both parts, but I had to pick one."

"I'm so proud of you, Bay." And I mean every word of that. Bayleigh is meant to be a star. She's gorgeous and so fucking talented.

"Thank you," she says as she tucks her hair behind her ear. "So one of them has us filming in multiple locations, but then the promotional tour and everything else for it will be like two to three years start to finish."

I nod and breathe. "What film is it?"

"Well, it's a big one based off of a book with a huge audience excited about the adaptation. It will potentially end up being a six to seven year ordeal.

"That's awesome," I lie, kinda. I mean, it is awesome, but it takes her away from me. I realized in the last few weeks I'm ready to settle down and have a family. I want that with Bayleigh, but it's becoming less and less attainable.

"It is." She looks away nervously.

"What about the other part?" I ask.

"Well, the other part is a role in a long-running series. Looking at eight to potentially nine seasons, depending on how well it does."

"That one doesn't sound as exciting as a huge blockbuster film." Before either of us can say more, I hear the bells on the back door jingling, signaling that one of the wiener dogs needs to go out. "I'll be right back."

I quickly make my way to the back of the house to open the door for the dogs. I leave it cracked so they can get back in when they're done doing their business.

When I get back, Bayleigh is scrolling through her phone. I stare at her for a minute, dreaming of all the things we could have had. I love looking at her like this, when she doesn't know I'm watching.

She must sense me there, because she looks over at me, then sets her phone aside as I sit back down. "Okay, where were we?" she questions, then remembers. "So, yeah. I had two choices to make. Be in a big blockbuster film traveling the world or a long-running series in one spot."

"I bet you picked the blockbuster film." I mean, that's what I want for her, kinda. I want her here, but I won't mess with her career, just like I know she wouldn't mess with mine. "When does it start filming? Do you get to go somewhere exciting?"

"Actually, no. I picked the long-running series." She smiles.

"Really?" I question, because why the hell would she do that? That doesn't make any sense. "Why?"

"Well, I realized my priorities in life have changed," she says matter-of-factly. "Let's go for a drive. I want to show you something."

She stands and starts walking toward the back of the house to let the dogs in. They're, of course, rolling in something in the grass. I roll my eyes, because they're about to drag grass into the house, but whatever. I'll clean it up later.

"Come on girls, inside." The second they hear her voice, they jump up and run to her. She pets and coos at them for a hot second before giving them a quick treat and leaving the sunroom.

I run and grab the keys to my truck before I decided to run back into my room and throw on a quick pair of jeans and a t-shirt. I slide my feet in some running shoes and then resume my trek back to Bay, since I'm sure she walked here from her mom's next door. "Where to?" I ask.

"Nope, I'm driving." She starts walking toward the front door, so I follow. I'm not one to argue with a woman on a mission. When we get outside, I see a brand-new car in my driveway. "I bought a car."

And it's the perfect car for Bayleigh. A cute, white Audi hatchback. I think it's one of those all-road ones like she's always talked about having.

"Niiice," I drawl.

"Thanks. I've always wanted one of these." She smiles.

"I know." We both make our way to the car, her to the driver seat, me to the passenger side.

When we're seated with seatbelts on, she begins backing out of the driveway. Things are still very awkward between us. I doubt they'll ever be the same if I can't have her to myself, but I guess this will do.

"Sooo…." She clicks her tongue to break the silence.

"Where are we going?" I ask.

"It's a surprise," she says, then opens the sunroof and turns on our playlist. The one we listened to when we were driving to Dallas after she became a runaway bride.

I laugh and watch her as she sings along to these songs we grew up with. It's a mixture of nearly every genre of music, because that's how Bayleigh rolls. She likes a little bit of everything. If you can't go from singing "Hot in Herre" to "Bohemian Rhapsody" to "Man! I Feel Like a Woman," you can't hang with Bayleigh.

She's so beautiful like this with the moonlight on her face, her full lips upturned in a small smile. She's happy, right here, right now, with me, and if that's all I'm ever going to get, then I'm going to allow myself to take it and be happy.

A few minutes later, we're pulling over on the side of the road near my parents' house. She unbuckles her seatbelt and gets out of the car, so I follow.

"What are we doing here?"

"This is what I wanted to tell you." She turns and looks at me.

"What?" I'm confused right now. Usually, I can guess what's going through her head, but this time, I have nothing.

"I took the series role," she says, and I just stare at her and blink.

"I know," I tell her. "You said as much at the house."

"Yeah, it turns out the series is being filmed at a studio in Shreveport," she explains.

Hang on a damn second. Shreveport. *Like forty minutes down the road Shreveport?* My line of questioning must be written all over my face, because she smiles widely and answers my internal line of questioning. "Yes, that Shreveport."

"Wait... so that means—"

She cuts me off before I can continue. "That I'm moving back home."

Before I can think of anything else, I walk toward her and slam my lips to hers, kissing her like my life depends on it. I pick her up and spin her around. She's moving back home.

Thank fucking Christ.

She pulls back and starts laughing. "Ace, put me

down." I don't want to, but I comply. She continues while she straightens her clothes and pats her hair back in place. "So I brought you out here to show you this."

"Show me what?" I ask when she doesn't elaborate.

"Well, if you'd give me a minute to explain, I could show you,"" she says.

"Sorry. I was just so fucking glad to have you in my arms again."

"This." She points to the field in front of us. I still have no idea what she's talking about. She sees my confusion. "I bought this land just a bit ago."

"What?" What does she mean by bought the land? This land is next to my parents', and they've been trying to buy it for years.

"Well, I put in an offer, and the owners accepted it." She pushes her hair out of her face again. The wind is horrible today.

"What do you mean?" I ask. "Why would you buy land out here?"

"Well, I called up Blake, my realtor friend, and asked him to look into who owned it. Turns out the owner passed away a couple of months ago. The land was then supposed to be split between his two children, but they decided they didn't want it, so they were literally about to put it up for sale."

I just stare at this woman, who is constantly surprising me. "Does this mean what I think it means?"

She nods. "Think Texas can handle me?" she asks

cheekily. "Because like Britney said, I'm back, bitch."

Holy fuck.

She's really back. Maybe not for good, but with eight to nine seasons to film, I'm thinking I can come up with a solid game plan to make her mine by then.

TWENTY-SIX

A BIG, BIG HOUSE

Bayleigh

"What are you thinking, Ace?" I ask. I need more from him before I tell him the rest of my plan. I can't tell what's running through his mind. It's like a million different emotions scatter across his face at once. Confusion. Excitement. Apprehension.

"I honestly have no idea," he answers honestly. "My parents have been trying to buy this land for years. I can't believe you were able to get it.

"Shit. Sorry. I had no idea." Fuck. I hope I didn't just fuck this up majorly by buying land out from under his parents.

"No! Don't be sorry. They'll be happy it belongs to you now." He grabs my hand staring out at the open field. "How many acres is it?"

"Roughly forty-five." I answer. The exact number is on the paper in the car along with the property lines, but I don't think that's important right now.

He just stands there quietly taking it in. I still don't think he figured it out fully. Men can be such idiots sometimes.

I give him a moment to come to the realization of what's going on, but when he doesn't I explain. "So I bought this land. I'm going to build a house on it."

He looks over at me and that's when he realizes it. "You're moving back home *home*?"

"I'm working with an architect to finish drawing up some plans my grandfather designed before he passed away. It's going to be modern farmhouse style." I walk to the back of my car and pull out a copy of my grandfather's rough plans. "Thirty-three hundred square feet, two stories, four bedrooms, an office, three bathrooms, huge living area, and a three car garage."

"Wow, Bay. I'm so happy for you." He doesn't seem very excited though. He seems to almost shut down again. Fuck.

"Ace," I call him by his nickname, but he just continues staring down at the house plans. "Archer," I say to get his attention. When he looks up at me I continue. "I want this *for* us."

His eyes get huge, actual realization dawning on him, slightly, but not completely. "What do you mean? Us?"

"I mean, that I'm moving back home because I realized somewhere along on our not-honeymoon that I could have the best of both worlds," I explain gently. And I'm going to, hopefully. Unless I've read everything wrong and he doesn't feel the same way.

I hope that's not the case. Not that it would change my mind about where I want to be in my career, but I don't know if I can live here knowing that we had a chance and I read the situation wrong.

This town won't be big enough for the two of us. And if he doesn't feel the same way I feel, I don't think I can live here. Maybe I'll just move to Shreveport?

Before I can continue that line of thinking Archer grabs my chin to look at him and begins kissing me like both of our lives depend on it.

We stop when a car drives by and someone catcalls out the window. "Fucking Rhett," Archer says.

"Rhett, like from school?" I ask and think back to the kid who licked bird shit off of his hands during our graduation ceremony. He didn't know what to do so he wiped it off with his hands but then when his hands were full and he had more to clean, he ate it. I still want to yark a bit just thinking about it. I always wondered where he ended up.

He nods. "He's such a damn idiot."

I can't argue with that, so we both just laugh and it's

the first time I think either of us have felt this carefree since *that* night.

"Where are you going to live while your house is being built?" He asks, shifting his feet like he's suddenly nervous.

"Probably with my parents or I'll get an apartment temporarily," I answer honestly. I haven't really talked to my parents about it yet either. So it really depends on if they're okay with having me there for a year or more. While I'm not real wild about moving in with them again, it's the best case scenario.

"Move in with me," Archer says suddenly.

Did he just say what I think he said? "What?"

"Bay, did you hear me?" I look up at him. "I said, move in with me." He did.

"Arch…" I begin, because that is the craziest shit I've ever heard. He can't possibly mean that. I mean, I know that I love him, I want this life, but we need to figure out our balance first. He puts a finger over my mouth to silence my verbal diarrhea so that he can speak.

"I know I've been a bit of an ass this past week," he says. I look at him like *ya think?* "I know. I'm sorry about that. I just didn't know how to handle it. I've been in love with you for years, Bay, only I just realized it recently." I open my mouth to speak again, but he doesn't let me. "Hang on, let me finish. I've been in love with you. I just didn't know it. And once I realized how deeply I felt for you, I knew that what we had was too important to ruin. I wanted to keep you in my life any way I could have you. I never knew if you felt the same way about me, so I just kept those feelings tucked away. I knew when you told me you were marrying Paul, that I didn't like it, I just never let myself think on the why. I knew I could never have you in that way."

"Archer..." I'm at a loss for words. How did both of us feel the same way and not know it? Is it too soon for us to move in together? This is new, should we take it slow?

"I know what you're thinking, Bay," he says gently. I'm sure it's written all over my face. "No, it's not too soon. We've known each other our whole lives. I didn't realize it then, but I think I've known it my whole damn life. You're mine, Bayleigh Hart. And I was made to be yours."

"I know. And I've felt the same way about you since we were kids. I've been in love with you, but I was never sure you felt the same way," I admit. "How can two people so in tune with each other miss this?"

"We hid it well. I know I did. Your friendship meant more to me than anything else. I didn't want to ruin it if you didn't feel the same way." He grabs my hands.

"Y'all didn't hide shit!" Grandpa yells from dad's tractor, making me laugh. "Glad to see you finally pulled your heads out of your asses."

"Should we be concerned about him on a tractor?" I ask.

"Yeah," he answers. "Honestly, probably."

"Goddamit Dad," I hear my dad shout from somewhere. "Get back here with my fucking tractor!"

"You'll never take me alive!" Grandpa shouts as he drives away with Dad hot on his heels in a side by side. "Suck my dick!"

"You sure this is the family you want to be part of?" he asks me.

"Absolutely. I bet Christmases are the shit at your house." I laugh. "Holy shit. So now what?"

"Now, you move in with me and we build a damn house. And soon I'm going to ask you a question that you're going to say yes to and…"

"And we'll live happily ever after." I finish for him.

"I was going to say I'll put my baby in you," he replies with a wide smile and pulls me in for another kiss. "Eventually."

He kisses me again and we let it get a little more out of control in our celebration. I pull back because we can't go further out here in the streets. I laugh at that thought though. "So who are we going to tell first?" I ask.

"Well if we leave now we can probably catch up with the high speed chase," he says. "My parents and everyone are right down the road," he points to the direction of their house.

"Evan probably needs to be the first to know. She knows about what happened on our trip."

He looks at me like he's terrified that his sister knows we had sex. "Oh God, *how much* does she know?"

I laugh. "Well, when she finally caught me at a vulnerable moment she asked what happened and when I went to tell her she plugged her ears and said she didn't want to know any details."

"Sounds like Evan." He puts his hand behind my back and guides me to the passenger door. "I'm driving, don't argue."

I shake my head, smiling. Such an Archer thing to do.

When he climbs into the driver's side after shutting my door he looks over at me and smiles. "Let's do this."

"Let's." I say as he pulls the car back on the road and heads toward his parents' house. We head toward family—our family.

TWENTY-SEVEN

Archer

"**M**an this car is fucking awesome," I say as I grip the steering wheel and rev the engine.

I look over at Bayleigh as she rolls her eyes. "Men and cars."

"Pfffft...you have no room to talk. You're the one that bought it." I reach over and grab her hand and it's like everything is right in the world. "My 1969 Mercury Comet is still better though."

She shrugs and agrees. "It will always be my favorite car. This one will be better gas mileage for driving back and forth to Shreveport though."

"Yeah it will." I smile and a few seconds later pull into my parents' driveway.

"Are you ready for this?" I ask her. It feels like years have passed by in seconds and huge life decisions were just made in half that time. I want this more than I've ever wanted anything in my entire life, but more than that, I don't want her to have any regrets.

"I've been ready all day," she says with a smile.

I jump out of the car and make my way around to the passenger side to open her door. It's a pet peeve of mine. No woman should open their own door. She unbuckles her seat belt and I hold out my hand for her. She takes it and climbs gracefully from her car. I shut the door and beep the locks on the key fob before pocketing her keys. I take her hand in mine and walk with her to the door, this time side by side. Right before we walk in and we both take a deep breath just before I push open the door.

The door opens right into the living area, though the sofas face away from it. Everyone is in the living room watching some television show, and when I say every-one, I mean my entire family. At some point in time, probably while I was making out with Bayleigh in her car, my dad chased my grandpa back to the house. Part of me wants to ask how that played out but then the other part of me knows that I really don't want to know. Also, we have important life altering shit to share with them and I need to get it all out before Bayleigh runs screaming into the night because most of the occupants in this room belong in a funny farm not a real one.

When the door opens they all turn around and see Bayleigh and I walk in together, hand in hand. And they cheer.

They fucking cheer.

"About fucking time!" Grandpa shouts.

"Tom!" Grandma says. "Language!"

"Is English no longer what we speak in this house? Should I learn French? German? Swahili?"

"No," she growls.

I hear my dad say "Finally."

And my mom says "Oh my gosh, we've been waiting so long for this to happen."

Evan wastes no time, she jumps up and runs over to us giving Bayleigh a hug first. I hear her whisper in Bay's ear, "I'm so glad it worked out."

"Me too," Bayleigh whispers back.

Evan comes back over to me and slaps me on the arm. "I'm so glad you finally got your head out of your ass, shit stain."

"Language," I whisper. "Or I'll tell Grandma."

"Tell Grandma, what?" Grandma asks.

"That Evan was just saying how much she'd like to meet a nice man now and how she just might have to take you up on your offer to meet your new friend's son," I reply.

"Oh what a nice idea," she claps. "I'll call Muriel

first thing in the morning."

"I hate you," Evan whispers.

"No you don't."

"Girl!" Grandpa booms as he calls for Evan's attention.

"Yes, Grandpa?"

"You better run before she gets her match making hooks into you."

"Good idea." She winks.

"And bring the tequila when you come back!" He laughs.

"I'm not coming back!" she calls out. "I'm moving to Sitka."

"Good luck with that, girl." He laughs. "She'll still find you though."

"You're right," she agrees with a heavy put upon sigh. "I'll just go find the tequila instead. It'll make the blind dates more palatable."

"Good idea," he says. "Bring me some too."

"I still hate you," she says as she passes me on the way to the kitchen. "But I'm glad you got your shit together. Be happy, big brother."

I shake my head, but with a smile on my face. She's not wrong. If Bayleigh and I would've just talked like this a week ago, we would have avoided all that bullshit.

"Y'all come sit down," my mom says. "We want to hear all about it."

And we do. Bayleigh tells them everything. From

the series she's going to be filming in Shreveport to the land she bought next to theirs. She was worried they'd be mad about her buying it when they've wanted it for so long, but they weren't.

"We're not mad, dear." My mom smiles, sweetly. "That land would've probably been Archer's anyway." She glances over at me. "Now it is, just in a different way."

My parents are nuts. They've always wanted me back out here instead of in the city limits. I was taking my time because I'm ninety percent sure Grandpa has a civil war cannon hidden somewhere on the property in an old outbuilding but I can't prove it yet. I wasn't sure I was ready to add my ring to this circus. I guess now it's time. I needed a sign and Bayleigh was it when she ran away from the altar at her wedding.

We continue chatting about the house plans Bayleigh has. She's showing them the plans her grandfather had drawn up years ago when he was in school for architecture. She even has a bunch of fixtures and stuff picked out already. She looks over at me though and says, "I mean, as long as Archer likes them too."

I just smile and nod, knowing that I will give her everything and anything she wants. I don't care about fixtures and stuff as long as it makes her happy. I would go to the end of the earth for her and now I get to spend the rest of my life showing her.

When we get up to leave to go tell her parents, my

dad claps me on the back. "I'm happy for you son."

Then he comes in for a hug.

"Thanks Dad."

A few minutes later we're pulling into her parents house. They're not sitting in the front living area like my family was so Bayleigh calls out to them. "Mom, Dad."

There's no answer.

She looks around a bit, knowing they're home because the front door was unlocked. "Oh they're probably on the back porch."

She was right. When we get to the door that leads outside we see her mom and dad sitting there, each enjoying a glass of wine.

When she opens the door she immediately says hi to her parents.

"Hey dear. Hey Archer," her mom says with a smile.

Her dad stands up to shake my hand. "You guys want a glass of wine?"

We both shake our heads and sit down on the longer outdoor sofa. "No thanks. Arch?" She asks.

I shake my head no. "I—we—wanted to talk to you about something."

"Finally," Mrs. Hart whispers under her breath and her dad is confused as fuck. I slightly laugh, but then get terrified because if we don't have his blessing we're fucked.

"Please tell me you aren't pregnant." Her dad sets

his wine glass down, I assume to gear up to kicking my ass, but Bayleigh laughs.

"Shhh Jack!" Mrs. Hart scolds her husband so Bayleigh and I can tell them we're together now.

"I have a couple pieces of good news," Bay starts out. She waits to see if her parents are going to say anything else, but when they don't she continues. "Well, I got a part."

"Oh that's good dear. Where is it going to take you this time?" Liv is excited and sad at the same time. "Are you going with her, Archer?"

She looks over at me and I look at Mr. Hart and he's so fucking confused. I try not to laugh.

"Uhh…" I say for lack of anything intelligent. Apparently Bayleigh played a lot of things pretty close to the vest this week. Not just with me but also with her parents.

"Here, actually," Bayleigh says softly.

"Here?" Jack asks. "What do you mean?"

"Well, I got a part in a new Netflix series they're filming in Shreveport. They anticipate it lasting about eight to nine seasons."

Liv screams, literally. So loud I think my eardrums busted. "Oh my word. Really? You're coming back home? For good?"

"Yes, Mom. For good." She smiles at her mom and dad. Her dad just stays silent waiting for the next piece of news. "Which brings me to the other thing." She takes a deep breath and grabs my hand. I sneak a peek over at her dad who is scowling. Fuck. "Archer and I are together."

"Fucking finally," Jack says. And I released the breath I didn't realize I was holding. At the same time Liv squeals again. "I knew it. Jack, I told you!"

"You did, Liv," he says sweetly as he pats her on the knee at the same time Bay and I look at each other, confused.

"What do you mean, you knew?" Bay asks. What the fuck is going on here? Please, for the love of all that's holy, do not let the people I have grown up with as second parents tell me that they know that I've fucked their daughter. I can take a lot, but I think that one might actually kill me.

"I told your dad when you ran away on your honeymoon that y'all would finally get your mess together and quit dilly dallying around," Bayleigh's mom explains. "He said I was just dreaming up what I wanted."

"That is not what I said, Liv." Jack side eyes her. "I said, let it happen on it's own. We've always known these two belonged together."

"Same thing, Jack. Same thing," she says with a broad smile and he just laughs and shakes his head. I guess after forty years of marriage, he just learned not to argue with her. Or he can't actually hear what she's saying to him anymore. Something about artillery and no earplugs.

I can only hope we love each other as much in forty years as we do now, howitzers and PPE notwithstanding. I look over at Bayleigh waiting for her to continue our plans. When she doesn't, I start, "I've also asked her to move in with me."

Her dad gives me a stern look. They're traditional and I can tell he's not happy about that happening without a ring on her finger. At least he's not about to talk to me about the extracurricular activities in Bora Bora. "I do hope you plan on marrying her then."

"I do sir," I reply back honestly. There is no reason to hide how I feel about her, not to anyone. It feels good to be able to say it out loud after spending the last few weeks feeling like everything I never knew I needed was slipping right through my fingers.

"Good." He gets up, I assume to grab more wine since his glass is empty.

Bayleigh decides to finish telling her mom about buying land and shows her the plans of the house, to which Liv starts crying because of what they signify. The plans her father had made.

Liv's father passed away of cancer a few years back, so anything honoring his memory is emotional for all of them. It makes me feel proud to know that we'll raise our kids in the house he had always wanted. I'm going to do my best to give Bayleigh everything she wants in that house. She doesn't know it yet, but she might have bought the land, but I'm going to build her the house she's always dreamed of.

I let them talk a bit as Jack comes back out with a bottle of champagne and two glasses. "I guess we should celebrate." He looks over at his wife who is fully crying now. "What happened?" he asks me on a frown, and I'm not ashamed to admit that my asshole puckered just a little bit at the change in his tone of voice.

"Bayleigh showed her the house plans her grandfather drew up, she's turning it into a house."

"A house?" he asks. He missed that part of the conversation, so I fill him in.

"Bayleigh wants to build the house that her grandfather designed on the land," I explain. "I'm going to do my best to see that she has everything she wants."

"That's great son," he says with a softness to his expression before he turns hard again and continues to make me sweat a little more. To be honest, I think he's enjoying it. "And I'm serious about that ring. Sooner rather than later now that you guys are going to be living together."

He gives me that stern, serious look and I believe he will have my balls chopped off if I don't follow through sooner rather than later. And as much as it scares me to have him concerned about the welfare of my balls, I'm actually okay with that. I can't wait to make her mine.

We've known each other for years, so why wait any longer? We've already wasted so much time—decades—when we could have just been loving each other.

When we're done celebrating with Bayleigh's parents we make our way next door. Bayleigh is champagne drunk, but is typing up a list on her phone of things she needs to get from her apartment in L.A. She said she left some stuff at Paul's place as well, but nothing important enough to ever talk to that bastard again. And for that I'm thankful.

I pull up to the three-car garage in my house, making a mental note to clean it out so we can fit her car in here with my two. For tonight though, we leave it. I park the car and walk around to the passenger side to help Bayleigh out before punching the code on the garage keypad for it to open.

I barely get the garage door shut when Bayleigh starts divesting me of my T-shirt. "I need you Archer."

And I agree. I need her too. I show her just how much, by grabbing the back of her neck and kissing her with everything that's in me. Everything that I've been holding back for years.

She reaches down to unbutton my pants at the same time both of us slip off our shoes. There's going to be a trail of clothing that leads to wherever she decides to land.

When we're completely divested of our clothing I realize we're in the kitchen. I look over at the counter and then to Bayleigh and smile.

She takes two steps back like she's about to run, but I don't let her. I take one giant step and grab her around the waist, pulling her to me. "Oh no you don't."

I lift her up on the counter and cage her in. *Mine*.

Bayleigh reaches around me and starts gently rubbing my back and my arms before landing at the back of my neck. This time she pulls me into a kiss. She holds me there while I take this time to rub her thighs. Teasing her one slow inch at a time as I get closer and closer to where we both want to be.

"Ace, stop teasing me," she whispers.

"But it's the best part, Bay." I slide my hands a little closer and she moans. I repeat the motion a few more times before she gets fed up and grabs my hard cock.

My hands instinctively go underneath her to pull her closer to the edge of the counter. Her hand rubbing up and down my length has me about ready to burst.

When she's all the way at the edge of the counter she lines my cock up to her and we both watch as it enters her slowly.

"Mmmmmm…" she moans.

I begin to pump in and out slowly until we get our rhythm and when she begins to move, I take her mouth in mine.

We devour each other inch, by precious inch.

This is right. This is the way it was meant to be.

Bayleigh is mine. And I am hers.

TWENTY-EIGHT

IT'S HAPPENING

Bayleigh

Two months later

Meetings. Meetings. And more fucking meetings.

I swear that's all these last few months have been. Well, mostly. I stare at the big rock on my finger and think back to the night Archer proposed to me a week ago.

"Where are we going?" I asked.

"To dinner." Short, sweet, and to the point, but that's literally all this damn man will tell me.

He had me get all dressed up, but refused to tell me where we're going.

When we pull up to our land I'm even more confused.

"Stay put," he tells me and I do as I'm told as he walks around the car door to open it.

Before he gets to my door, he opens the back door to retrieve a bag out of the back. When he opens it I see the top part of my boots peeking out. "What are you..."

"Just go with it," he says and hands me the boots.

I take off my heels and slide the boots on. Luckily the dress I'm wearing looks good with both.

When I'm done he puts the bag and my heels in the back seat and reaches his hand out to mine to help me out of the car. He closes the car door and we start walking on the dirt road that's there as a makeshift driveway for now.

Construction of the modern farmhouse started last month. Right now it's just a bunch of dirt work to level out for the foundation but it's progress.

When we get closer to the house I see a blanket laid out with a basket. A picnic? He got me dressed up for a picnic?

Still holding my hand, Archer leads me over to the blanket and I realize it's a bottle of champagne and two glasses.

"What's going on Ace?" I ask.

He turns and faces me and gives me a quick kiss before starting his monologue. "You and I have known each other all of our lives. I'm sure our parents have pictures and videos of us making mud pies in the back yard in our diapers.

He takes a deep breath and nervously runs his fingers through his hair. I don't interrupt though, I can see where it's going and I begin to shake. This is it. Oh my gosh, it's happening.

"They say the best marriages start out as friends and I really hope that is the case for us. I've known for years that you were it for me, but just never really knew how to express that and I'm so sorry about that." He reaches up and swipes a tear from my face as I shake my head. We were both fools. Such idiots who didn't face their feelings for twenty years like idiots.

He gets down on one knee. "And I mean that. Bayleigh Hart, will you make me the happiest man in the world and be my wife?"

I'm speechless, but I nod letting him know that I want nothing more than to be his wife. His forever.

He lets out a breath when I wipe the tears from my eyes so I can see what he's holding. It's the most perfect ring in the world. His grandmother's ring. A ring from a long-lasting marriage. And it means everything in the world to him—and me.

He places the ring on my finger and that's when I see the photographer come out of the tree line a few feet away. He's truly thought of everything.

He reaches down and kisses me before saying "I love you."

"I love you too," I reply. And I mean every word of that.

We take a couple of pictures with the photographer then he takes my hand. "We have one more stop."

We make our way back to the car when he tells me I can put my heels back on or leave the boots on. I opt to leave the boots on because they actually do look cute with this dress.

A few moments later, we're pulling into his parents' house and I laugh. "Gotta tell your parents?"

He smiles and squeezes my hand. "Something like that."

When we walk through the front door it looks like no one is home, but the lights come on when Archer screams out, "She said yes!"

And everyone cheers. They're all here. His parents, my parents, his sister, his grandparents. Everyone.

It was truly one of the best nights of my life.

Now we're in full wedding planning and house building mode, all while getting used to my new co-workers on set.

Life truly has a way of working itself out and I couldn't be happier.

EPILOGUE

ONE IS THE LONELIEST NUMBER

Evan

"So I found the cutest little bakery in between Sunnyville and Tall Pines," Bayleigh says to me. "It's called *Land Sakes Cakes!* Isn't that adorable?"

"Oooh," Archer butts in. "Do you think she has carrot cake? I love carrot cake."

"I'll make sure you have whatever you want, honey," she says to him as I mash the limes down in my seven and seven with my straw. "This is our special day."

Carrot cake? Who even likes carrot cake? Sometimes I swear my brother was switched at birth. He's so weird.

Don't get me wrong, I love him. He's my best friend. So is his fiancée, Bayleigh. I grew up tagging along with them on their adventures. But now… now it feels a little like I've been left behind.

I'm happy for them. I've never wanted two people to get their shit together more than these two and that's really saying something because I do not need to hear my girl or anyone else wax poetic about my brother's penis. EVER.

But there's also a part of me that has recently been reminded that I'm alone. Everyone is coupling off and I'm still here by myself. Usually that doesn't bother me. Grandpa Tom would tell me to stop being such a girl. Crying is for pussies and all that. Even when Archer shot me with a BB gun. That hurt like a bitch and grandpa just said "Girl! Don't you cry on me." But lately, I can't help but feel… emotional. God that word is gross.

"Evan?" Bayleigh asks, shaking me from my thoughts. "Are you listening?"

"Yes," I answer even though we both know that's not true. "Maybe? No. I'm not. I'm sorry. I guess I just have a lot on my mind."

"What's going on, Ev?"

"Nothing really," I reply. "It's true. I have the cutest class this year and new-to-town student. He's so precious I would seriously consider a kidnapping if I didn't have an aversion to federal prison."

"So that's what's really bothering you?" my brother asks. I can't tell him what's really going on, that' I'm jealous of what he has, what everyone around me seems to have. I swear last spring when Pastor Frank said, "Be fruitful and multiply," the people of this town and the surrounding areas took that as a challenge. It seems like everyone I went to school with is engaged, pregnant, or has just had a baby.

But not me. One really is the loneliest number.

"The new Superintendent is a real hard ass," I answer and it's not a lie, he is, just not to me. I haven't even met him yet and I probably won't either. Why would he be? I'm one kindergarten teacher. He has much bigger fish to fry than how we learn our letters with Umber the Umbrella bird.

"Has he given you a hard time?" Archer asks and I realize my misstep. I should not have told my protective big brother that my new mean boss was scary.

"No," I reply quickly. "Nothing like that. There's just some rumors circulating. Besides, you know how well liked Dr. Conners was. Anyone who came in and made waves was going to hit some push back."

"Then what made you upset?"

"I don't know," I lie. "I guess I'm just not feeling like myself. You know how I feel about conflict."

"The more bloodshed the better?" he asks and while that's true I try and demure.

"Yes, usually but not in front of the children."

"Your sister is going to be the craziest aunt ever," Bayleigh says.

"Are y'all pregnant?" I practically screech.

"No," she snaps. "And keep your voice down. You know how people like to talk."

"I'm sorry," I reply. "You scared me."

"And you scared half the county with that scream," she says.

"True. I should probably get going," I tell them. "I have glue projects to grade."

"How do you grade a glue project?" Archer asks.

"Wouldn't you like to know?" I snark, sticking out my tongue.

"Better watch it or your face will freeze like that."

"Good, the better to scare your ass with."

"Love you, Evan," Bayleigh says as she hugs me tight. "Don't be a stranger."

"Never. Thanks for dinner."

"Anytime."

I head out of the tavern that they had asked me to meet them in. It's not in Sunnyville, but the next town over, Tall Pines, and is family owned. The fried chicken basket is so good, I can look the other way that their football team, the War Eagles, beat our Bulldogs every time. They do have a coach who made it all the way to the Super Bowl when he was younger though. That's practically cheating and everyone knows it.

I climb in my car and head home to my cat, Diablo.

If I'm going to embrace my spinsterhood, I should at least do it with a bad ass cat, right? And he is a badass.

I unlock the front door of the townhome I rent and head straight for my bedroom at the back of the shotgun style house. I strip out of my clothes and pull on a tank and a pair of leggings because everyone who's anyone knows that home is where the real pants are not.

I pad back to the kitchen and pull open the side-by-side fridge and freezer doors. I could eat my feelings and down a pint of rocky road, or I could drink a glass or two of the new pineapple wine I picked up at Walmart the other day with my groceries.

"Merow," I hear from behind me.

"Hey buddy, what'll it be?" I ask my furry friend.

"Merow."

"You got it," I reply, plucking the bottle from the shelf next to the can of tuna with the little purple Tupperware lid sporting a happy kitty face on the top. "Wine for me and smoked tuna for you."

I pull a glass from the cupboard as he jumps up on the counter where he likes to be fed. He's getting up there in years and it's harder and harder for him to move around but he still does it even if he's a little worse for the wear.

"Merow!"

"I know. I'll be right there," I tell him and I should have known that wine was not more important than nighttime tuna because he is one unhappy kitty.

"Merow!" he wails as he reaches out a paw and shoves a box of corn flakes that I had left out right off the counter. And I will swear to God that he looked me right in the eye while he did it too, that little bastard. Gosh, I love him.

"Fine! Have it your way!" I shout back. I set my glass down and pull a clean bowl from the next cupboard over. I set it down in front of him and pop the purple lid off the already opened can. I spoon the fish flakes into his bowl and watch him happily gobble them up. He might be getting old, but he's still got some living left in him.

I grab the broom and dustpan from the corner and clean up his temper tantrum with a side eye for my favorite kitty. I toss the mess in the kitchen trash and then grab the wine opener, only to find that the bottle has a twist off cap. Am I classy or what?

I pour until the large bowl of my glass is full and I grab the bottle and head into the living room at the front of my town home. I settle into my favorite corner of the couch and flip through the channels until I find a *Real Housewives of Dallas* marathon. Those are my favorite ones! They're so funny and sassy. I just love them. For a month straight, Bayleigh and I would shout how tired our pantiliners were whenever we saw each other.

My wine is crisp and sweet with bubbles, a lot like drinking a fancy seven up. I let myself forget about my troubles for a bit with some mindless television and eventually, Diablo comes in and settles on my lap. It helps that I have his favorite throw blanket with me. He sleeps wherever that blanket is whether it's his for the taking or not.

Before I know it, the bottle is empty, the marathon is over, and I'm wondering why I can't get a man with an eye patch to love me. I'm Evan Stone. I don't need a man to decide that I'm worth it. And fuck everyone's damn FacePlace updates! So you're in a relationship, good for you! You got engaged? Awesome! But I don't need your internet validation. Or do I?

And then the most brilliant idea hits me. I should get my own damn FacePlace update! Just like everything else in this world, I can't wait on someone else to get done tomorrow what I can do my own damn self today.

I grab my phone off of the table next to me and flip through the apps until I pull up the FacePlace app. I thumb over to my profile and hit the edit button. I change my status from SINGLE to IN A RELATIONSHIP but it asks me to tag the person in question.

Well damn, I don't have one. That's okay, I'll choose my own.

"Eenie meenie mighty mo, pick a feller by his toe. If he hollers, let him go. My momma said to pick the one with the biggest penis and I choose you!" I sing song as I scroll through the names of the people I might know and land one that seems familiar but I'm not sure why. "This one. I pick you, Mack Whitlock. Congratu-

fucking-lations. I just changed your life."

And then I drop my phone beside me and pass the fuck out.

The End!

Just kidding.
To be continued…

ABOUT THE AUTHORS

Jennifer and Alyssa are besties immersed in the publishing world. Owners of LitUncorked and Blush Magazine, they said they'd never work together, but their lives are now so intertwined, when a book idea hit both of them they figured the next perfect step was to write a series together.

FIND THEM AT

www.jenniferrebecca.com
www.alyssakale.com
www.lituncorked.com
www.blush-magazine.com